A LONG JOURNEY HOME

WINSTON H. HUNT, PA

LIGHT SWITCH
PRESS

Published by:
Light Switch Press
PO Box 272847
Fort Collins, CO 80527

Copyright © 2017

ISBN: 978-1-944255-70-1

Printed in the United States of America

DEDICATION

This book is dedicated to all veterans who served this great nation in times of war. The book is especially dedicated to the estimated 2.7 million veterans who served in country, and in the combat waters, during the Vietnam War. Over Fifty-eight thousand, of America's youngest and brightest military personnel paid the ultimate price. Some bravely served aboard Huey Choppers, volunteered for hazardous missions, fought in rice paddies, and crawled through the jungles that made up the country. There are approximately 800,000 thousand of us who are left to continue our "Long Journey Home."

It is also dedicated to all the support personnel who kept the war supplied with everything they needed to succeed, and to the thousands of men and women still fighting wars with physical and emotional wounds. Maybe in some small way those who read this story will find encouragement to persevere and never give up.

TABLE OF CONTENT

PREFACE

The innocence of growing up in the rural south is threatened when Hank decides to leave home. His life is forever changed the day his family drops him off at boot camp. Some would say excerpts from his letters home reveal two extremes. Those to his family were upbeat while those to his brother describe the rest of the story.

Hank's long journey home begins when he is involved in a helicopter crash in Vietnam and suffers catastrophic injuries. He is treated at several Army Hospitals and Veterans Hospitals on his return home. He suffers from post war depression and battle fatigue while trying to deal with the loss of his crew members. He seeks to make something of himself by helping fellow veterans who are suffering both physical and mental wounds.

EARLY TIMES

If you wanted to find Hank Weatherspoon during the summer, just venture out into the countryside around Willacoochee, Georgia. Look for a tall stand of long leaf southern pines and listen for the sound of chainsaws or the strain of a loaded pulpwood truck making its way out to the road. Hank and his family should be nearby. Hank started going out with his father, uncle, and older brother at a young age as they harvested lumber for a local wood preserving company. Hank was the "choker" on the crew. He was responsible for attaching a chain called a choker to the cut down trees and hooking them to a machine which would move them to the trucks waiting to haul them to the mill. When Hank wasn't attaching logs, he would go searching for arrowheads and other artifacts left behind by the Indians and traders who frequented there years earlier.

The Indians and traders followed the Alapaha and Willacoochee rivers which flowed through the county. The Alapaha is what is known as a blackwater river, which flows below bald cypress, long leaf, slash, loblolly pines and majestic oaks, covered in moss, on its way to Florida. Black water rivers are usually slow-moving and flow through forested swamps or wetlands. As vegetation decays, tannins leach into the water, making a transparent, acidic water that is darkly stained and looks like tea or Coca Cola. The Willacoochee is a black water tributary of the Alapaha, joining it near the town of Willacoochee. If he didn't find any artifacts, Hank would go hunting. He would look for quail, squirrels, rabbits, turkey, deer; whatever was in season. He'd take his prize home where his mother would cook it up. Many times, she had put together the best quail, hushpuppy and coleslaw meal you would ever put in your mouth.

Life in Willacoochee was great for raising a family, however, making a living in the area was getting tough. There just were not a lot of opportunities for teenagers like himself to pursue so most of the young people moved on after high school. Hank was only thirteen, in 1963, and was already wondering what he would do in Willacoochee for the rest of his life.

Willacoochee is located in a part of southern Georgia known as gnat spitting country. You cannot take a breath in the summer without spitting gnats out of your mouth or swatting them from around your eyes and nose. The town grew up on the Alapaha River and along the railroad which connected Brunswick (on the east coast) and Atlanta (the state capitol). With two rivers flowing through the county, the land was fertile for row crops, fishing, and hunting.

Hank's grandfather, Bert, had raised his family on a small ten-acre tract of land outside town. The house was a one-story Sears, Roebuck and Company catalog home. It had three bedrooms and two baths. He had purchased the home and the land from his job driving a sand truck for a local sand company. The sand was mined from the banks of the Alapaha River and sent by rail throughout Georgia, South Carolina, Alabama, Florida, and Tennessee for use in the construction industry. Bert was short in stature and often found himself fighting off bullies who nicknamed him "Shorty" during his younger days. Despite this, he was a gentle loving husband and a great grandfather. He had certain routines which included always cleaning up before supper and wearing a tie to the table. After supper, he would retire to the parlor and listen to the radio or read the paper in his favorite chair. He really enjoyed listening to Braves baseball when they moved to Atlanta in 1965. They quickly became his favorite team and he listened to as many games as he could. Before bed he'd pick up his Bible and read a little.

Bert's wife was named Myrtle and she looked like the perfect grandmother. She was petite, kind of plump, whitehaired and had a smile that could melt butter. She was always cooking up a mouth-watering meal. She would start her days off collecting the eggs, picking vegetables from the garden (when in season) and then going in to the kitchen to start supper. Coming home to a house full of supper aromas would make your mouth water. Supper was always a grand time because everyone was there and they enjoyed each other's recollections on the day. After supper, Myrtle, Harriet, his mother, and Jane, his sister, would clean up and then head for the parlor. Myrtle would pick up a knitting project and quietly sit listening to the radio. She too would then read some from her Bible before going to bed.

Hank's father, Jim, was almost six feet tall and in pretty good shape for a man in his fifties. He had spent most of his youth helping his dad Bert haul sand, and later joined his brother Willard in the logging business. Pine and cypress timber was an important resource in South Georgia since the pioneer days and almost every South Georgia town had a sawmill and turpentine operation. Jim and Willard eked out a modest living hauling trees to the local wood preserving plant.

Hank's mother, Harriet, was kind of short, stocky and full of personality. She was an elementary school teacher and the families' biggest cheerleader. She was also an excellent cook and, like Myrtle, enjoyed putting on a big spread anytime she could. She enjoyed working in the family garden and feeding the chickens. She tried to send the family off every morning with a full stomach which usually included fresh eggs and biscuits.

Jim and his wife, Harriet, had a separate bedroom added to the family home after they married. Their evenings were spent like just about everyone else's, except for one difference: Harriet might grade a few of her students' papers or set up the next day's class schedule, while Jim would just sit and reflect on a good day's work. He might even talk about going hunting on the weekend.

One day, Jim surprised the family when he walked in carrying a window air conditioner. This was the first air conditioner the family had owned. He put it in one of the parlor windows, since this was the room used the most in the summer.

Hank and his sister, Janet, would spend most of their evenings doing homework while listening to the radio. In their own special way, each was thinking about life outside of Willacoochee.

Purvis, Hank's older brother, was twenty years old and still single. He was almost six feet two inches tall and had brown eyes, brown hair and was tough as nails from handling a chainsaw. He had played offensive tackle and defensive linebacker in high school. He had caught the eyes of some college coaches in Valdosta, Georgia, until the day he had a terrible accident. He was in wood shop at school one day and lost three fingers on his left hand while operating a table saw. This ended his hopes for playing college football. At the same time, the accident might well have been a blessing since he was classified "4F" in the draft. Despite all this, he was doing well working with his dad and uncle.

Janet, Hank's sister, was nearly eleven and sort of a plain Jane. She played the flute in school but also felt trapped in Willacoochee. She thought she might end up teaching school like her mother and that really bothered her. Listening to the radio in the evenings had made her want to see the world outside of Willacoochee.

Hank was thin, strikingly tall and well muscled from working in the family pulpwood business. He was a fair student and ran high school track. During the summer, he usually got a sun burned red neck from cutting lumber from sunrise to sunset. He and the rest of the family were proud to be known as hard working 'red necks'.

Uncle Willard, Jim's brother, lived down the road a piece with his wife Irene. They had been married several years and never had children. Willard spent his early years helping Bert and Jim mine sand from the Alapaha river before starting to work for the local wood preserving plant. He would later join Jim, who had started his own logging business harvesting wood for that same plant.

Sportsmen from all over the south would come to the area drawn by its abundance of game and fish. There was deer, turkey, rabbit, dove, and quail everywhere. Fish of all kind could be caught in the two rivers flowing through the area. If that wasn't enough, you could attend one of the rattlesnake roundups in nearby Cairo, Whigham, or Bainbridge. Feral hog hunting was becoming a popular sport. The wild hogs rooted in the rich bottom land of the rivers. They would destroy acres of land and crops in no time. It was always open season on these rooters.

A local grocery, gas and grill store was located a few miles outside of town that served up the best all-the-way hamburger with fries for miles around. You could always combine the burger with a Coke, grape Nehi, sweet tea, or a cold beer. A couple of pool tables with overhanging Budweiser lights added to the mood. Pool sticks hung on the walls for those who didn't bring their own. Stools were scattered around the tables for patrons' viewing. There was a jukebox in the corner loaded with all the Hank Williams, Willie Nelson, Johnny Cash, and Dolly Parton tunes just waiting to be played. A couple of booths set the boundary for a small dance floor.

On Friday nights, you had to get there early because the owner served up his specialty steaks served with a baked potato, salad, and beverage of your choice. It would get so smoky in there from the grill, cigarette and cigar smoke that your date's perfume had to work overtime just to compete with it. Several floor fans ran 24/7 trying to keep the air breathable.

One day, while cutting some limbs off a felled pine tree, Hank's chainsaw kicked back and cut a large gash in his left lower leg. He was taken to a nearby hospital where the cut was cleaned and closed with several stitches. The physician in the ER began talking to him while putting over fifty sutures in the leg. He, of course, asked Hank, "How did this happen?"

Hank replied, "I was cutting limbs off a tree when the chainsaw kicked back."

The doctor answered, "You were lucky. You could have lost your leg. Why don't you think about doing something else while you're still young? There's not much of a future in pulp wooding, you know."

Hank agreed but asked, "What else is there to do around here? I'm helping my father, uncle, and brother in the family timber business."

The doctor replied, "Why don't you think about joining the military. I joined the Navy shortly after my father died unexpectedly. I was about your age-nineteen or so. I had to drop out of college because I didn't have any more money. If I had not joined the Navy, I wouldn't be the physician I am today. I went to the Navy Hospital Corps School in Chicago, Illinois, as a young reservist. I used the GI bill, reserve pay, plus money from a part-time job to go back to college and then medical school."

Hank replied, "Really, sounds pretty cool."

The physician continued, "While on active duty in the Navy, I got three meals a day, uniforms, a good salary, health and dental care along with paid vacation time. Think about it this way. If you join the military at eighteen, by the time you're thirty-eight you could retire with full benefits. Everything I just mentioned plus the GI bill, a VA loan for a home and retirement pay would be yours. You'd be set for life and young enough to even start a new career if you wanted."

Hank thought it over before responding, "Sounds pretty good to me. I didn't even think about the military, especially with a war going on."

"That's a good point," the doctor added. "But if you join now instead of maybe being drafted, you could most likely pick the branch of service you want and the type of training you want."

The doctor had opened Hank's eyes to another world outside Willacoochee. He remained at home through the summer and thought daily about traveling around the world with all expenses paid. Sure, there was a war going on but maybe he could beat the draft by joining early and he could pick where he wanted to go. He began to dream about what he could do after serving his twenty years. The urge to start a new adventure began to materialize.

He knew it would be difficult to leave his family, but it was for the best. He began researching the different military branches and talking to Purvis about what he was thinking.

"The Navy has good food and bases located around the world in a lot of cool places," he told Purvis.

"Yeah", Purvis replied, "But crossing an ocean in a ship doesn't sound all that appealing to me. What if it sank?"

Hank, "You have a point there. That would be my dumb luck, and I don't swim that good either. Can't you see me floating on a raft in the middle of some ocean?"

Purvis asked, "What about the Air Force?"

Hank responded, "I thought about that. The Air Force also has good food and bases, but the very thought of flying on one of those large planes we see coming out of Moody Air Force Base just doesn't appeal to me. I just don't see how something that big stays up anyway."

He added, "Maybe I will join the Marines. I'm pretty good with a rifle and really dig those dress blues. I can see me with a girl on both arms. Girls like men in uniforms, especially Marines."

Purvis answered, "Yeah man, but that's where all the action is right now. Maybe you'd get shot or something."

Hank said, "I thought about that and think this chainsaw injury would keep me out of making it through boot camp anyway. So, it looks like I'll be joining the Army."

"Cool," said Purvis. "There are plenty of bases here in the south for you to choose from; Fort Gordon in Augusta, Fort Stewart in Savannah, Fort Benning in Columbus are all close and you could come home on weekends."

Hank's decision became easier when his uncle Willard was killed suddenly after his logging truck ran off the road. The police officer mentioned that it looked like he swerved to miss a deer, or something else, and lost control. The trucked flipped and he was crushed under the weight of the heavy logs. So, on his eighteenth birthday, Hank became the first member of his family to join the military.

After Uncle Willard's death, Purvis found himself spending a lot of time at Aunt Irene's house. Willard and she never had children so he found himself helping with the chores and doing minor repairs. She often told him how much she appreciated his help. She even suggested that if he ever married they could move in with her. The house was a modest three bed room, wood frame structure that sat on fifteen acres of land.

BOOT CAMP

In 1968, Hank enlisted in the Army and was sent to boot camp at Fort Jackson in Columbia, South Carolina. Boot camp was a great maturation of young men from all over the country coming together for eight weeks of Army training.

While in boot camp he only had time to write a couple of letters home. One was to the family expressing how well he was being treated and how strong he was getting:

"The first place they took us was to some kind of a reception area where we got our uniforms, had our hair cut off, were given all kind of test, a dozen shots for all kinds of diseases, and had a personnel file started. You should see me with short hair. They treat us all the same, like we are nothing. It's all in an attempt to build us up into the Army way of doing things. We're up before sunrise and go to bed well after sunset. The food is good and I can do fifty pushups in my sleep. We are marching miles every day and learning how to shoot rifles and machine guns. Keeping your weapons clean is top priority. Kind of reminds me of cleaning my shotguns and rifle back home. 'Keep your weapons clean and dry', the sergeant keeps yelling at us. Hours are spent cleaning our M-16's until it can be broken down and reassemble in the dark. The drill sergeant just keeps yelling at us, like we are hard of hearing. All in all, it's not bad. I sure miss your cooking and evenings in the parlor. See y'all soon."

Hanks mom and dad wrote back, "---We're proud of you. Bet you look cute with your hair cut off. What kind of diseases do they think you can catch? Keep it up. Will you be coming home after boot camp? Come home soon. Everyone at church is asking about you."

To his brother, Purvis, who helped him pick the Army and get him into this mess, he wrote:

"The moment I arrived on base my life was changed forever. I am told when to get up, when to shower, when to eat, and when to sleep. The days last from sunrise to sunset. I've become physically reduced to nothingness and gradually re-strengthened into the Army way of doing things. Any recruit who showed up undisciplined quickly becomes disciplined. Those who showed up boys quickly become men. Those who were loners soon learned how to depend on others.

"We're learning how to save a life with first-aid and how to take a life through self-defense and weapons training. We're learning how to think as a group and function as one. We're being trained to go to war and how to survive that war. It's been eight weeks of hell and those drill sergeants just keep yelling at us while wearing those damn Smokey the bear hats.

"We probably won't get much time off unless we do extremely well. There is no TV, but we hear students at Allen University, Benedict College and the University of South Carolina are staging sit-ins and burning their draft cards. It doesn't sound like many of us would go into town anyway. I've got the feeling guys with military haircuts aren't welcome in town.

"Oh, one other thing. There's a salvaged Huey helicopter here which they put on the top of a twenty-five foot, wooden tower. Guess I will be jumping out of it when I go through evacuation training. Something else I have to look forward to is what they call fire and movement techniques, whatever those are. Will write more later if I have time."

Purvis wrote him back, "I won't tell Mom and Dad that it's not all fun and games up there. You will get through it and I'll learn not to pick a fight with you anymore. Sounds like you're ready to kick ass. If you do get some time off, don't be chasing down any USC coeds."

The family drove up to see him graduate from boot camp. It was a grand day full of excitement and a simulated battle. There were helicopters dropping GI's out on the enemy and a firefight erupted. One squad hit an enemy mortar team with small-arms fire as another moved up the enemy's flank. Explosions blew up enemy vehicles. Moments after the assault, the crowd started to cheer. It was a decisive victory, as drill sergeants and trainees emerged from the battle scene.

Hank took the family on a tour of his living area and some other base facilities. They spent the most part of the day making small talk and excited for Hank graduating. They all knew where he most likely was headed from here. He told them how he wanted to become a gunner on a Huey helicopter and help protect GI lives by providing cover and rescue operations. The day went by fast, and when it came time to say good-bye, a few tears were shed. They all promised to keep in touch as the family loaded into the car for the return trip home.

After boot camp, Hank was sent to Fort Campbell, Kentucky, where he would learn how to clean, shoot, tear down, and reassemble a M-60 machine gun. He would learn to do it in his sleep. He was being trained to go on over to Vietnam, along with hundreds of Americas finest and brightest young men.

Hooah!!!

VIETNAM

From Fort Campbell, Kentucky, Hank was sent to a helicopter unit stationed between Da Nang and Hue, South Vietnam. He volunteered to be a gunner on a Huey (UH1) gunship. The gunner was a person who fired a machine gun, usually a M-60, and provided cover for missions. There were three other crew members; a pilot, the aircraft commander, who would take over the flying if something happened to the pilot, and another gunner. The UH-1's were also being used on a multitude of missions such as transport missions, medevac missions, supply missions, and shuttling VIP's around country.

Medevac missions became known as, "DUSTOFF" missions. Early on, the medevac choppers didn't carry weapons, but as Charlie (North Vietnamese) obtained more sophisticated weapons, they were outfitted with M-60's for defense. The life expectancy for a medevac crew landing in a hot LZ (landing zone) was usually 30 seconds, and if mortars were launched it was reduced to less than 9 seconds. All medevac crews were volunteers because of the high risks involved. Those crew members who served more than one tour were thought to be 'certifiably insane'.

Gunships provided additional coverage for Dustoff missions and for units on the ground that needed help fighting off the enemy advances.

The Huey had a distinctive flat hollow thumping/whomping sound which was produced by its rotors. That sound became the sound of Vietnam. A Huey could be heard long before it was seen and soon became the image of the war.

Hank's crew was led by the main pilot, Robert, who was a lieutenant and on his second tour. He told Hank, "I came over in September 1967 and have flown several hundred missions during my time so far. I've flown all types of missions from Dustoff, VIP, transport, weapons replenishment to gunship missions. I will take care of you. It's going to be fun."

Alvin asked what a Dustoff mission was and Robert said, "It stands for Dedicated Unhesitating Service To Our Fighting Forces." He then continued with his introduction, "I'm from Rochester, Minnesota, and I still feel out of place in this damn hot and wet country so far from home. I'm married to Kelly and we have two daughters, Heather and Jennifer. I want to work for a civilian medical transport company when I get out of here, flying choppers."

Dain, was the crew's warrant officer and commander. He introduced himself to Hank as being from Lubbock, Texas, and also being on his second tour. "I had been a crew chief during my first tour in '67 - '68 and I applied for the warrant officer pilot training program at Fort Wolters Army Base in Mineral Wells, Texas. It was one hell of a training program but I made it. Welcome aboard, we're all going to make it back home," he added.

He said, "I'm married to the most beautiful twenty-two-year-old gal you'll ever see. Barbara has olive colored skin and dark eyes and hair. She teaches special education at one of the middle schools. We don't have any children yet, but we want several," he concluded.

Alvin introduced himself as a gunner like Hank, "I'm from Dothan, Alabama, and was drafted into all this mess. This is my first tour. I got here a couple of months ago and I'm looking forward to serving with you."

"Hank, why don't you tell us about yourself," they said.

'Well, there's not a lot to say, I'm from Willacoochee, Georgia," Hank responded.

"Now wait a minute," Robert said. "Willacoochee, where?"

Hank said, "Willacoochee, Georgia. Give me a break, guys. It's a small town in South Georgia near Moody Air Force Base in Valdosta. I joined because I didn't want to get drafted and I got sent over here anyway. Let's get some chow."

Later on, Alvin told Hank, "My mother is a home seamstress and a devoted Christian who regularly attends an AMC church near Dothan. My dad is called Buck because of his physique. He is a big, muscular, tough looking dude who works as a mechanic for a local car dealership. He has big plans to open his own garage one day and wants me to join him."

As the crew got closer together, they spent hours talking about family, children, wives and girlfriends. Heck, no subject was off the table. Once Alvin recalled, "I used to watch the Dothan Cardinals play home baseball games in Wiregrass Memorial Stadium with my dad. They were a local, all black team and were pretty damn good."

"I love baseball," Hank added. "I spent many a night listening to the Braves playing on the radio on the Braves Radio Network with the family sitting in the parlor."

Alvin went on to say, "I grew up in the middle of segregation and couldn't eat in the same diners as the white folk. I couldn't sit in the same doctor's waiting room. Heck, for a long time there were separate hospitals and separate schools. We even had to use separate restrooms."

"I know. Remember, I'm from Georgia," Hank said. He then asked, "Did you see Dr. King's march in Selma or the church bombing in Birmingham?"

Alvin answered, "No. Stayed pretty much at home. It wasn't safe to wander too far away. I was in the middle of it all, though. Rough, rough times."

Alvin was on a roll, "Man, I would answer a job advertisement and be turned away because of my color. I only had a high school education, no working history, and was from the wrong side of the tracks. I could only pick up odd jobs at some of the local farms."

Hank tried to change the subject, "Did I ever tell you about skinny dipping in the rivers back home?" he asked.

Alvin, "Not yet, I can't wait."

"Well, it had to be a moonless night or the girls wouldn't take their clothes off. You never knew what you'd come up with in your arms after skinny dipping. You just hoped you were kissing your date and not some damn catfish," he laughed.

They both retired for the night with their M-16's close at hand. Hank liked to write home at night because thinking of home helped him to forget about where he was.

In one letter, he wrote about the base:

"Phu Bai is a large base located south of Hue along highway 1, in Corps I, central Vietnam. Just look for Da Nang and then up to Hue and we're to the west. It's a big base with wood two story barracks for us enlisted guys, metal buildings (Quonset huts) all over the place and tents everywhere you look. There's a heavily bunkered hospital which stays full and a chapel which is equally full. At times, it's hard to believe we are in the middle of a war zone. There are officers' clubs, NCO clubs, places to see movies and stages for USO bands to play on. There's even a Sargent's club.

"The locals wear silly looking hats that are shaped like upside down ice cream cones. They are made of grass or straw and help shade them from the sun and rain. They are worn by the farmers and peasants mostly. The women in towns tie them on with different colored cloth, maybe it's some form of a fashion statement. They even wear sandals made out of rubber tires. The soles are made from the tread and the straps from inner tubes. A lot of guys are sending them home as souvenirs.

"When I left base the other day, it was like stepping into another world. Little people were scurrying everywhere with no place to go. They walk bent over, heads down in a sub-missive way. They would bow as they passed. They appear broken down from the years of war and poverty. I couldn't help but feel a mistrust between us. After all, we had invad-ed their country. They live in houses built out of bamboo, mud or straw. Most have thatch, tin, recycled tarp or straw roofing. As many as four generations live under one roof. Some families live in the streets and have no real sanitation. Smells from open fires cooking cabbage, noodles, rice, veg-etables, and maybe even snake meat fill the air. The aroma of food cooking helps cover the stench of no real sanitation. Animals run free along with small children chasing after them. Thick areas of bamboo are built around most villages to mark boundaries. It is so primitive over here. I was glad to get back to the base.

"In the cities like Da Nang and Hue, the picture is dif-ferent. People ride around on bicycles, motor scooters and have all kinds of transportation. They look like ants traveling in different directions. Everyone is catering to the military. They work in hotels, night clubs, and restaurants, all bidding for the GI dollar. There all girls on every corner who want to be your friends.

"The locals who work for our government, or private contractors, do pretty good. Word has it they get three dol-lars a day constructing buildings which tend to be shelled shortly after completion. I guess it's a form of job security since they get paid to build them back again. Not bad when you consider the average annual income was three dollars a year before the war.

"The Germans have a hospital ship, in Da Nang, which only treats civilians. When Da Nang is going to be shelled by rockets or mortars, she sails out of port. It took our guys a little while to figure out what was happening, and they started to send some of our ships, like our own hospital ship, out of port when the German ship went out."

In another letter home, Hank apologized for the delay between letters.

"It seems like every time I try to write you all, a mission comes up or I get interrupted by RPG's hitting the base. I learned the other day that if you have been in country thirty days, you can take R&R (rest and relaxation) anytime during your year tour. You can take up to seven days and go to places like Hawaii, Japan or Australia. Maybe if I stay, I'll go on R&R. Seriously, who would want to return to this place after seven days in Australia?

"They even give you a yearbook when it's time to go home and everyone is buying Zippo lighters and other souvenirs. Kind of reminds me of boot camp.

"The base floods so much that some guys use inflatable boats to get around. It seems to rain every day. All in all, it's not bad over here. See you soon. Maybe I'll call y'all soon."

He later wrote Purvis;

"Security fires defensive night flares to light up the area making sure nobody (sappers) is crawling into camp. NVA/VC sappers would penetrate a perimeter in advance of a ground attack by other NVA/VC units. They would start a battle from within. At the same time, another unit would attack from outside the perimeter. Charlie sappers would get naked and put grease on their bodies, allowing them to crawl through razor and mangle foot barbed wire like it wasn't even there. I don't think I'll ever get used to the ground flares keeping me at that night. There is every kind of aircraft that the army has over here. Huey's, CH-53'S, CH-54'S, C-130'S, C-117'S, Army Mohawks, and C-47's can be seen everywhere. We're flying several missions daily and drawing fire on almost all of them."

Purvis was starting to see a pattern here. Hank was telling one story to the family, usually about how great things were, and another entirely different story to him. It was like a tale of two cities. He decided to show his dad Hank's letters. Both agreed to keep them away from his mother. She was worried enough as it was.

One Sunday after lunch, Hank told the guys about what his family did for the 4th of July. "The men folk in my family would gather around a large iron kettle which was big enough to put a hog in. We'd pick a hog out, kill it, and split it up the middle to gut it. Then we'd put it in the kettle for cleaning. The water would boil the hair off the skin, and then we'd put it over a wood fire pit and slow cook it all night long."

Robert and Dain interrupted, "Get out of here, sounds cool!"

Hank continued, "The scent of the hog cooking would bring neighbors from far and near. We'd sip on a few cold ones while waiting for that sucker to cook. During this time, we'd share old hunting stories from years back. One neighbor would always tell the same story about old Kenny's coon dog 'Cutter'. He'd tell us year after year how old 'Cutter' chased a coon all night long and didn't come home for two days because he was plum worn out and then he'd laugh real loud.

The group replied, "Sounds like a pretty good time and a very long night."

Hank didn't stop there, "When the hog was ready, we'd cut it up and all the family would eat some of the best, most tender barbecue you'd ever put your mouth. The meat would just fall off the ribs."

Dain chimed in, "Thanks, now I'm hungry again. Sounds great. Let's eat."

"Wait a minute guys. That's not all." Hank added. "Later on, in the day, we would sit around and eat some watermelon. We'd see who could spit the seeds the farthest. We'd play horseshoes and maybe a pickup soft ball game."

Robert said, "Sounds a like a great time and a good way to celebrate the Fourth. All we usually did was watch the parade in town. Then go home and listen to a baseball game and later watch the fireworks. Last year, here in Nam, it was work as usual with the night flares for fireworks."

To help pass the time Hank and Alvin found themselves drawn to the Huey. They had befriended the crew chief who worked on their Huey. He was more than glad to teach them the ins and outs of that bird. Danny was on his second tour and told them about how temperamental the Huey was. "They all have tube engines which run hot and you have to take them up 11,000 to 13,000 feet to where the air is cooler and bleed the engine off," he told them.

He added, "Taking off from inside a bunker can be tricky. The rotors cause a downdraft which bounces off the ground and the sand bag walls of the bunker. This causes a terrible swaying action. You have to work the foot pedals hard to keep it steady, otherwise she'd go in circles and maybe hit the sides and crash."

Alvin said, "Sounds tricky. Robert just gets in and up we go. I never thought it was that difficult and dangerous. And to think I want to become a crew chief one day."

Danny kept telling them, "Don't walk on the left side when she's running. The tail rotor just might take your head off. I've already seen this happen too many times. You young guys just don't seem to listen."

Hank sent another letter home:

"When we're not out flying a mission or spending time with Danny, the mechanic, there's always a volleyball game,

touch football, or basketball game going on. We played a
lot of "Acey-Deucey" and just talked about girls, or started
filling sandbags. There's always something to do.

"I even told the guys about how we cooked a hog on the
4th of July, drank a few beers, told a few stories and watched
you women folk sitting around spreading the latest gossip. I
told them how the kids would play hide and seek, catch, or
tag, and how we'd all go to town to see the parade; how we'd
look at the model A's, listen to the high school band, watch
the horses pass by and the Shriners drag racing their go carts
in figure eights. I told them we did about the same thing for
Veteran's Day and New Year's."

He wrote Purvis about the first time Alvin said he had sex. "He
told me he had met a sweet young girl at church and after several
youth trips and fish fries, he took her down to see an old sleeper car
at the train depot in Dothan. 'We choo-chooed all night long,' he
told me. Said he still misses the train whistles every now and then.
Got to go! The base is being shelled."

The next morning after breakfast, Alvin said to Hank, "I wish
they would cook up some red eye gravy with grits every now and
then. That would really hit the spot. By the way, when was the first
time you ever did it?"

"Did what?" Hank replied.

"Oh man, you know what we were talking about last night. The
first time you did it with a girl," Alvin responded.

"Oh that!" Hank answered and proceeded, "I was fifteen when
I went skinny dipping for the first time. Man, she was so hot. She
had brown hair and eyes and a body to die for. Her breasts were like
full, round, firm honey melons. Her complexion looked like a true
Georgia peach in full bloom with no blemishes. We sat on the beach
along the Alapaha River watching the sun go down. Then we went
in for a cool dip and from that day forward, she called me "Uncle

Wiggly". I had to get away from her as fast as I could. Another reason to join the Army.

Alvin, "Don't blame you at all, man, not at all 'Uncle Wiggly'".

These remembrances would go on and on between missions because, when there wasn't a mission, things could get pretty quiet.

Many a night was spent going to bed praying you would sleep all the way through. It also helped if you thought about home before trying to sleep. Hank would go to sleep remembering how beautiful the quail sounded at sunset. Robert would often think about his daughters and what they were doing. In the morning, you would awake to business as usual in beautiful Phu Bai. This scene played out every night, unless it was payday or the first of the month, when Charlie would mortar the base until 12 or 1 am just to let you know they were there.

Robert shared a letter from home about his two girls. "Heather is 12 and plays the trumpet in the middle school band. Jennifer is 9 and is a cheerleader. Kelly is busy doing mom things and has painted the bedroom again. I think that makes three times this tour. On my first tour, she painted it five times. Says she wants to keep it looking cheerful for when I get home. She's turning into a pretty good plumber, electrician, and painter since I've been over here. Man, I really miss them."

Dain said, "Shut up man! I think I'm going to cry. You're making me home sick."

Dain and Hank were checking out the Huey one day and started talking about Lubbock, Texas. "You know, I went to most all the Texas Tech football games. Living in a college town has its advantages. So many young things running around town, especially on game days" Dain told Hank.

Dain went on to say, "I'm convinced that there are UFO's out there because V -shaped lights had been seen over the city in 1951."

Hank replied, "Get out of here. There's no such things as UFO's."

Danny chimed in, "What about Roswell?"

Dain said, "See, I told you they were out there."

Hank kept asking Dain, "Which state produces the most cotton?" Dain answered, "Texas, of course. Lubbock is the largest cotton-growing region in the world according to the chamber of commerce."

Hank said, "I don't care what the chamber of commerce says. I still believe it's Georgia."

Alvin, who was always close by added, "Personally, I think it is Alabama."

They were interrupted by VC rockets and picked up their M-16's on the way to the bunkers. Danny kept telling them not to worry," They don't have anything right now that reaches this far into the base, as he kept on working on the Huey.

The food was less than desirable. It seemed like roast beef was served every day. To make things worse, there were small bugs in the bread. After another boring meal served on paper plates, Dain threw out a question, "Why do countries fight each other?" "What the hell are you talking about now?", everyone asked.

Robert was the first to answer, "I think countries go to war to impose their own values on others."

Hank answered, "Nope it's purely for economic reasons like gaining more borders, sea side ports or maybe rail service."

Alvin said, "I think it's for money. We're here because of the gold. We don't care who controls the gold just as long as it's not the communists. Vietnam produces a lot of gold and they don't care how many people are killed just as long as they keep control of the gold. It's all about money."

Dain chimed in, "Guys cool down, I really don't care. I just thought I'd ask the question."

About this time the mail came and Hank's sister, Janet, had sent a package full of sweet things. She sent some cookies, canned fruit, nuts, canned tuna, canned chicken, chewing gum, and candy. It was a good day until incoming rounds started hitting the base.

The next morning Alvin told the group that he had written his family last night to send a care package. "The cookies and stuff from Janet, yesterday, sure were great. Maybe we will get some more treats soon." Dain added that he also had written Barbara the same thing in hopes of her sending something good, too.

Robert and Dain were sharing some thoughts with the crew about their first tour in Nam. This war is changing rapidly into one big political war. They told about how several hamlets back in March of '68 had been attacked by GI troops trying to rid them of VC inhabitants. Several hundred civilians had been killed during these attacks and the brass really caught a lot of heat over it.

Robert told them, "Nam is unlike any other war in American history. In previous wars when our guys took an area, or town, the front line moved with them. Everything behind them was considered secure and presumed safe. Not so here. Our guys would take one area, or village, only to find out that sappers would come out of their tunnels, or other hiding places in the villages and ambush them from behind. There are no front lines over here. The villagers are friendly to our guys when they are in the village and just as friendly to the VC when they are in the villages. It's been their way of self-preservation since this country was first occupied,"

Dain added, "You just don't know who is your friend or foe and if the people back in the states would understand what was happening, they might not be so quick to label us, 'Baby killers'. I heard at Wolters during my pilot training that a Lieutenant was going to be tried for the actions of his platoon during that time in March of '68. We've gotten into one hell of a mess over here."

The days turned into weeks and then months. During all this, the stress was starting to build for everyone. Several missions a day, along with daily mortar attacks and night time flares, were starting to wear the guys down. Alvin found himself not wanting to participate in the daily discussion groups as much. He was no longer trying to figure out what was going on. He seemed to be withdrawing and could not forget what Robert and Dain had said about the war and civilian killings. Hank had noticed this change and asked him, "Hey, what's up with you lately?"

Alvin responded, "What do you mean?"

Hank replied, "You aren't yourself lately, anything wrong?"

Alvin didn't reply, so Hank backed off hoping that whatever was bothering Alvin he'd be able work it out. Meanwhile, Alvin was starting to sleep less, if at all. This was concerning to his buddies, since each counted so much on one another during missions.

Hank shared his concerns in a letter to Purvis:

"Hey bro, Alvin is really starting to crack. Racial tensions are increasing and we've heard about all the demonstrations state side. Are people really calling us 'Baby-killers?'

"Morale is dropping off daily and there is less leadership. I hear officers are being shot just because no one wants to follow their orders. Why are we here? I hope, Alvin hasn't started to smoke pot or try speed. It's everywhere and easy to get. It's getting bad, really bad over here. We've been doing three or more missions a day."

Hank finally approached Alvin again. "Hey, why don't you level with me? What's bothering you?"

Alvin answered with several questions, "Do you ever think about where your rounds are hitting? I mean we're firing all we have into elephant grass, triple canopy and villages all the time. What are hitting? Are we hitting the enemy, kids, civilians, or even our own guys? Are we taking innocent lives or what?"

These questions were way too heavy for Hank, but he answered the best he could. "We're doing what we've been trained to do. To protect the guys on the ground. I don't know where my rounds are hitting either, I only know I'm trying to save my brothers. I try not to think about it. This war has been going on for years and if the locals don't know how to seek cover by now, there's not a whole lot I can do about it. It's either them or us and I want to go home." Alvin didn't say anything and just walked back to his bunk with his M-16.

Hank overheard an air-medic talking to his buddies about a GI he'd picked up. He was sweeping a village and as he entered a hooch, a young girl about four years old pulled the pin on a grenade. Instantly, he shot her and while doing so he saw his own daughter. It really tripped him. They found him wandering around the village saying, "I killed my daughter, I killed my daughter". Hank thought how glad he was that Alvin wasn't with him to hear this tragic story and hoped that GI would recover from his mental wounds.

They were awakened for a night mission south of Da Nang near Quang Ng Ai. Apparently, all hell was breaking loose as VC sappers had penetrated a battery LZ perimeter setting off satchel charges and hitting the place with mortars. The guys in the battery needed some air support and medevac help.

The next morning at breakfast Dain commented, "That was one hell of a party last night. Did I ever tell y'all about this gal I met back home called Cathy? She was my first love."

"She was thirteen and a cheer leader in my junior high school. She had blond hair, green eyes and was just about to bud out in full bloom. She stole my heart away the moment I saw her. I let everybody know I loved her and was going to marry her. She was my first love but she apparently didn't feel the same about me and broke things off. Unfortunately for me, The Everly Brothers had just released a song, 'Cathy's Clown', and I got so tired of hearing them sing, 'Here he comes, that's Cathy's clown' that I vowed to never date another girl named Cathy." Everyone at the table just laughed.

Sometime later Robert told them how he met his wife Kelly. "We met during the summer of my second year in college. I was sitting in a Humanities class when this girl came in late. The only seat open was beside me. She was so hot and I was so lonely. After a few days of small talk, she invited me over to her home for lunch. I followed her home like a puppy. Her mother, Connie, was waiting for us and we had lunch by the pool. Her dad showed up about an hour later. He usually went home for lunch and a nap each day. He ran a hardware store with his brother, on the main street in down town. It had been in the family for years and they were keeping it afloat despite all the big box stores moving into the area. Kelly's brother also worked for the store along with about six other people.

"Her father asked me if I wanted to go for a swim in the pool? I told him I didn't have any swimming trunks and he said there were some in the pool house. What a day I had meeting her mom and dad.

"I continued to visit Kelly's house and within six months I asked her to marry me. She answered 'Yes,' so we went inside and asked her parent's permission and they gave it. No, she wasn't pregnant. We set a date for six months from then and never looked back."

They got a mission to fly to an artillery fire base on Dong Ap Bia Mountain west of Hue. Apparently, the NVA had launched a surprise night attack in an attempt to overrun the fire base and our guys need-ed a lot of help. This was in the same area where our Airborne troops had started to encounter heavy resistance trying to take a hill. All the artillery guns on the fire base were destroyed by the enemy and our troops were having a hard time taking that hill.

Hank found himself getting scared of missions. He was a naive kid when he went to Nam and just wasn't prepared for the experi-ence. He was not used to seeing so many wounded GI's with the kind of wounds they suffered. He had helped load and unload ampu-tee patients his own age. He had seen head wounds, chest wounds, and burns so bad that he later lost his cookies. He went to Robert to talk about it. He asked Robert, "Do you ever get scared?"

Robert responded, "Oh hell yes, every time I take off I'm scared. If you're not scared, you're not human. How are you supposed to react living in a combat zone? I even say a few prayers during a mission. We all want to go home in one piece and I'll do my best to see that happens. It's going to be ok."

The mission they had flown to the artillery fire base on Dong Ap Mountain, reminded Robert of one he had flown about a year earlier. "I was called to fly a medevac mission. We were so short of pilots that most of us flew any time we were needed. I had to fly into an area north of Saigon known to have VC tunnels. Several of our guys had been pinned down and needed help. The LZ appeared to be secure enough until I was about fifty feet above it. Then, all hell broke loose. My gunner, Ted, and the medic were giving it all they had. Their M-60's were spitting out rounds so fast the muzzles were turning red. I managed to get the ship down, pick up a load of wounded and get the heck out of there. After we returned to the base, we found that the Huey had over thirty holes in it. It was one hell of a ride. I knew my time wasn't up after that mission and said, 'Hail Mary full of grace,' more than a few times!"

The guys were silent and could only say, "Damn."

Hank had just enough time to send Purvis a letter:

"Hey bro, hope you are good. For the past five days, we've been flying multiple missions daily supporting our guys on a mountain southwest of Hue. It's the middle of May and our guys have been catching it for four days now. Apparently, they are trying to get a bunch of NVA off the top.

"It is difficult to reach the top because of steep dense terrain and enemy bunkers. They are rugged mountains covered with bamboo, tall elephant grass and sometimes double and triple canopy. The NVA are throwing everything they have at them. They are even coming out of tunnels.

"We are flying day and night, any type mission they need, just to keep on top of things. All the MASH units and hospitals are filling up with casualties, including the hospital ship REPOSE off shore. Don't know how many times we've taken wounded out to her. This has to be the biggest thing going on in the war so far. I bet it makes headlines around the world.

"I don't know how long this one's going to last but feel real worried for our men stuck up there. Sorry, I can't tell you more because the mail is censored, so just watch the news. The media is all over this one. I got to get out of this place. Things are starting to crumble. Write you soon."

Hank was getting real homesick and told the guys, "Back home, in the fall and winter months, most of our attention turns to Friday night high school football. Football in the south is pretty big stuff and we usually had a fair team. That didn't stop us from getting together on Friday nights and filling the stands. It was the weekly social gathering."

Dain said, "Texas has some pretty good high school football games on Friday nights too. I know what you mean."

Hank continued, "The strongest team in our area from year to year is Valdosta. I can't remember how many regional and state championships they have won, but it is a lot. We'd drive over from home to watch their playoff games, since Valdosta was only about thirty miles away."

In a letter home, Hank wrote that he had told the guys about what the family usually did on Saturday's in Willacoochee. I told them how hard it was to find a parking place in town. I told them how all the families would drive to town to do their weekly shopping. How we wore our best clothes and made it sort of like another excuse to catch up on local gossip and see the neighbors. Then I told them that after shopping we'd usually go home and watch a college football game.

It was time for another mission, this one was to give cover for a radio unit drawing fire north of Hue. It was an overcast day with a strong chance of rain. They were headed north east toward the DMZ. All the missions were tough especially flying over rough territory. You had the feeling there were snippers in every tree that had a bullet with your name on it.

Packages from home were getting more frequent and larger. The families were learning what shipped well and what didn't ship well. Alvin's mother had gotten the hint from his last letter and sent some peanut butter, crackers, and pretzels. Janet, Hanks sister, sent more chewing gum and candy. Roberts wife started sending jams, cheese crackers, and lemonade mix. She even sent a box with bourbon balls in it. After months on the South China Sea, they were ripe! Dain's wife sent SPAM, crackers and Texas Pete Hot Sause.

"SPAM, that's right, what about it? What does she know being home all alone? If you don't want it I'll be glad to eat it," Dain said.

In an effort to change the subject, Hank asked the group if he ever told them what we did on Sunday's back home.

"No, but I'm sure you're going to tell us," answered Dain.

"Well, on Sundays, we'd all go to church in our Sunday best. Afterwards, we'd go home for lunch; fried chicken, ham, baked yams, corn bread, and mac and cheese were the trusted staples."

"Dain said, "Shut up man. You're making me hungry."

"That's the truth, guys, and after lunch we'd sit around on the porch or watch a pro football game on TV."

Robert said, "That's the good life; damn I miss home."

Hank went in to write a letter to his family:

"Thank you for the care packages, all the guys families are sending them now. We're getting all sorts of goodies. Dain's wife sent some Texas Pete, which we put on everything, along with some SPAM and crackers.

"You know, the people are real poor over here. They live in shacks or straw huts. Some even live on the streets. They mainly eat rice and raise most all of their food, including animals. They cook outside in open kettles, like we sometimes do on the 4th, or just over open flames. They are always smiling and bending from the waist to us. Most of them just seem to be running around like chickens with their heads cut off."

The next night he wrote Purvis:

"Since our last big skirmish, when all hell broke loose on Dong Ap Bin, we hear from the states that people are criticizing the war, the military and military values. We are hearing about college students burning draft cards and several demonstrations protesting the war. Meantime, morale is dropping fast here. Seems there is no interest in winning anymore."

Hank got a letter from his mother:

"Dearest Son, I look forward to your letters. You are giving us quite the tour of Vietnam. I almost feel sorry for the conditions they are living under. Everyone here is well. Your dad and Purvis are hard at work cutting trees. My school work is keeping me real busy and never seems to end. Sister Janet is always complaining of too much home work. When Purvis isn't working he's over at Aunt Irene's helping her with the chores and minor repairs. She's told him that as first born she plans to give him the place and the fifteen acres.

This has really helped to motivate him. I packed some goodies and you should get them shortly. Let me know what you
want and I'll try to send it in future packages. Love you and
pray for your speedy safe return."

Robert shared some more memories from his first tour, "I remember shuttling VIP's between Saigon, Long Binh, Cam Ranh
Bay, and Da Nang during Bob Hope's Christmas special in 1968.
Bob Hope came over with Raquel Welch, Barbara McNair, and Les
Brown's Band of Renown. In Da Nang, the hills were covered with
marines and GI's from all over the region. Guys were hanging off
power poles and even crawling under the stage. No one knew better
than Bob Hope just how much laughter means to a GI so far away
from home. His shows always ended with the singing of 'Silent
Night'.

"I even took Miss America and some of her court out to the
Hospital Ship REPOSE, along with numerous other USO bands
during my first tour. The wounded and sailors always looked forward to those visits. I just missed being the chopper pilot to mark the
10,000[th] safe helo landing on board, since she arrived."

"When are we going to get some missions like that?", Alvin
asked. "I hear Billy Graham even came to Da Nang."

"Won't be too long now. I know they are already making plans
for this year's tour."

Alvin went up to Hank and said, "Remember the day we were
talking about flying VIP's, Miss World and Ms. America all around?
It got me to thinking. What would your perfect women look like?"

Hank answered, "She would have full cheeks with a complexion
to rival any prize- winning Georgia Peach. Her breasts would be
firm and about the size of small honeydew melons. She'd be about
5'-8" with a waist small enough to wrap my arms around. Her hair
would be blonde, short and she'd have brown eyes of course."

Alvin said, "Man, what a girl."

Hank replied, "So, what would your perfect girl look like?"

"Dude, she'd be about my height with a small waist. Her hair would be dark and she'd have crystal clear brown eyes. Her teeth would be white as snow and her lips soft and tender. She'd have breasts about size 34 D and they'd be firm, not droopy. Her legs would be thin with perfect knees. You know, without faces on them, and when she walked, she would hold the eyes of every man around."

Hank," Man, she sounds like a beauty queen."

Alvin was real excited one day, shortly after mail call. "Look at what my dad sent me. He showed them a picture of a 1953 Chevy panel truck he'd just purchased that he wants us to restore when I get back. You know, he really wants me to join him when he opens his own garage. Just think what this will look like with a few modifications."

Robert said, "Like putting a big block 350 cubic- inch V-8 in it with a four- barrel carburetor."

Dain, "And maybe a posi-traction rear end with automatic transmission."

Hank, "Put a hot red color on that bad boy with duel exhaust, mag wheels and maybe drop it a few inches. It would look awesome, man, a real lowrider."

Alvin, "That sounds bad guys. I'll write dad back with all your suggestions. It really would be one cool ride."

Alvin's spirits seemed to pick up some after getting the letter from Buck. He was real excited and wanted to know what everyone's first car was. Robert was first to go. "It was a 1954 Oldsmobile 88 two door without the post. My dad used to fly and on the way to the airport we would pass a house with that Old's sitting under a car port. It was turquoise and white. I told dad I wanted that car and lo, and behold, he bought it one day. It had a big block V-8 that sucked gas like water. I didn't care since gas only cost about .25 cents back then. That car just seemed to fly down the road. Alvin, what was your first car?"

"I didn't really have a car. Remember dad worked for a car dealership as a mechanic and didn't make a lot of money. The family did have a '59 Chevy Biscayne station wagon that they let me use. The panel will be my first car."

Dain chimed in," Mine was a 1960 Henry J."

"A what?", Robert interrupted.

"A Henry J made by Kaiser-Frazer Corporation. It had two doors and wasn't much bigger than a shoe box. It looked like a turtle with a hump back and long hood. My dad and I painted it bright canary yellow and rebuilt it. It was a 4 cylinder with three on the tree. I didn't keep it long because of all the flack I was getting driving it. Say Hank, what was your first car?

"I didn't really have a car either. Like Alvin, our family only had one vehicle and they let me drive it every now and then."

The earlier conversations about their first cars reminded Robert about what his dad, Mike, had done one time when they went flying. Remember, it was on one of the previous trips to airport that they first saw the Old's. His dad had been taking flying lessons for about six months and asked Robert to go up with him. He was learning to fly a single engine Piper Cub that was painted yellow and only held two passengers. One passenger sat in the front, while the other sat behind. The plane had a stick in the front and one in the back to move it up or down.

Mike put Robert in the front seat and flew the plane from the rear seat. He took off without a hitch and was practicing touch and goes. The day was clear and there were no turbulences. During one of the circles, Mike took the Cub straight up and stalled the engine. As the plane fell, nose down, all Robert could see was the ground coming up fast. It scared the stew out of him and he held onto the two metal bars which were holding the windows in. He started yelling because he thought he was either going to fall out or crash.

His dad restarted the engine and began to pull it out of the dive. Robert didn't fly with him for several months after that. He laughed out loud thinking about what his dad would be thinking of him fly-ing a Huey in Vietnam.

About six months later, Mike had to fly across the state on busi-ness and asked Robert to go. Well, by this time, his dad had moved on up to a four seat Piper Tri-Pacer. It was bigger and much faster than the Cub and they'd only be gone one day.

It was a beautiful day when they took off for the trip. The sky was blue and there wasn't a cloud anywhere. Visibility was ten miles with a favorable tail wind. They had no trouble flying to the meet-ing. After the meeting, they learned that afternoon thunderstorms were expected to build near home and decided to spend the night and fly home in the morning. They didn't have any toiletries, any sleep wear or a change of clothes.

When they took off the next morning, they had clear skies for about twenty miles when they ran into fog. It was so heavy that it made seeing the ground almost impossible. Mike wasn't instrument rated but it was daylight and the fog shouldn't last long. They flew on a couple hours and Mike was getting worried. He estimated they were about forty miles from home and he really needed to find a break in the fog to see where exactly they were. A break finally ap-peared and he was able to confirm his location. About fifteen miles later they were out of the fog and landed safely. Robert flew only one time with him after this flight.

It always seemed they were talking about how they missed home. Alvin used to say, "I miss my mother's cooking. Mom could really cook up a spread; ham, potato salad, coleslaw, and fresh baked bis-cuits that would just melt in your mouth."

Robert would tell how he missed the smell of perfume in the house. "Each of my girls wore a different brand of perfume. It got to where I could tell who was in the room without even seeing them. I also miss the neighborhood kids playing on the sidewalks."

Dain was always going around telling everyone how much he missed football games. "I'd go to a high school game on Friday night and a Texas Tech game on Saturday every chance I had," he'd tell them.

Hank would say, "I miss the sound of the trains coming through town at all hours of the day or night. I often laid in bed wondering where they were going and knew the direction from the sound of the horns blowing. I would even dream about the hobos riding on them and where they were going."

All of a sudden, the base was being hit by missiles, RPG's and incoming rounds. This time, Danny even headed for the bunkers. Charlie was letting everyone know he was still alive and kicking.

Later the next day, Hank walked up to Alvin and said, "I think you should paint the panel a two- tone blue."

"What are you talking about man? Get a life, blue is for sissies."

Hank's mother wrote him with some bad news. His grandfather, Bert, had been working the garden one day and felt some chest pain. He was in his seventies and had suffered a heart attack. He spent a couple of days in the hospital and was doing fine now. "We didn't want to bother you until we had more news. He is back home and Myrtle is hovering all over him."

Hank couldn't help but feel anything but relief at the news. Still, he wished he could have been there to help out. The memories from childhood times spent with Grandpa were flooding his brain. He shared the news with his buddies who tried to console him by listening to some of his memories.

He told them about the time Bert took him deer hunting. "He let me take a 30-30 caliber rifle along that day. We left a little before dusk and headed for his favorite spot out back on our property line. He perched me in a tree and told me not to make any noise. I sat there hoping to see a deer and kill it. All I saw instead was a couple of rabbits, some squirrels, some turkeys, and a few quail. I got bit by ants and mosquitoes and never saw the first deer.

"Another time, he took me fishing to one of his favorite places on the Alapaha River. He put bait on my hook and I sat for a couple hours without even so much as a nibble. I never had much luck hunting or fishing with him, but we sure had fun. He was the first to let me drive his truck. He put me on his lap and I drove all around the property."

All his buddies said they were glad Bert was going to be all right. They tried to reassure him that the two of them would have time for many more memories when he got home.

Later that night, while he was trying to fall asleep, he remembered how Grandpa used to tell some whoppers. The family would be sitting on the porch when Bert would just come out with a story. He remembered him telling them about the time the revenuers arrested old Jessie. Jessie had a still down in the swamps of the Alapaha River which looked like a jungle in places. You could get lost pretty easy if you weren't familiar with the area. A lot of people made shine to supplement their income especially during the depression and old Jessie made some of the best.

The Federal boys had come in to the area to sweep the moonshiners out. There was a lot of demand between Tifton, Waycross, and Macon, Georgia, for good shine. One of the feds decided the best way to find the stills was to use his nose and ears. He set off into the swamps and found a place to sit down. Then he just listened for the crackle of a fire and smelled the air for that sweet mash aroma. He picked up the scent of a still and followed his nose right up to Jessie's still. He found Jessie filling up glass jugs with the clear product. It was a fine still which produced some of the best shine the revenue man had ever tasted. He told old Jessie how sorry he was to have to shut him down and suggested that when he got out of jail he should try to find a way to make it legally. He said old Jessie told him that, "That wouldn't be no fun. Shucks, half the fun is trying to outsmart y'all!"

After a few more days, Robert walked up to them with good news. "I started filling out my 'girly calendar' today. I'm getting short. September isn't far off now. Won't be long before I'm boarding the 'Freedom Bird' and heading home."

Dain said, "I'll be right behind you."

Alvin said, "Let me see that calendar. Cool man, real cool. I like where they put the last day."

Hank added, "Beautiful. Seems like I just got here and I'm already looking forward to starting my own calendar. Damn, I still have some time left in this hell hole." He then went in to write his family about Robert's good news. "He's an ok guy. Y'all would like him. He said he might visit us when we get home."

Hank then wrote Purvis a letter:

"I hear the guys in the jungles eat C-rations which come in brown cans. They heat the cold meat with pinches of C-4 because most of the time no heat tabs were packed. Some go months without taking a shower. They live under triple canopy with the insects, poisonous snakes, which they kill with sawed off shot guns, and burn leeches off their bodies with cigarettes. The enemy is all around them and calls out at night hoping to keep them up. They even fire small arms off along with flares making for restless nights. As if that's not enough, the monkeys and parrots make all kinds of weird noises. Our guys don't have dry socks and several have developed immersion foot, better known as jungle rot. Many have to be medevac'd for cellulitis.

"Back here on base, I can't even cross the compound without thinking that every local I pass could be a sapper. You know, they are trained like our Rangers and Navy Seals. They are really a bad bunch of guys, those sappers are. Hope this ends soon.

"Drugs are everywhere. Marijuana is grown here, like cotton, and a lot of guys are experiencing it for the first time. Heck, speed and pain killers are being handed out like candy. How are those guys going to cope when they get home? I want to get out of this place."

THE JOURNEY BEGINS

The day started off like any other day. It was clear, cool and there was a hint of orange color in the sunrise. Breakfast in the mess hall had the usual scrambled eggs, hash, muffins, and dark thick coffee to wash it all down. Dain and Robert attended the morning briefings on what they could be expecting during the day. They would receive the weather forecast and any possible missions. Robert's crew was called up provide air cover for a medevac mission north west of Phu Bai, up near an old abandoned French Fort in the Quang Tri District. The crew piled into the helicopter and each member went through their pre-flight routine. Alvin and Hank checked their guns, while Robert and Dain obtained the coordinates and warmed the Huey up. Everyone was reminded to stay clear of the left side of the chopper while it revved up because no one wanted anybody to get hit by the tail rotor.

Robert said, "Ready for lift off. We're headed for a pinned down patrol near the base at Khe Sanh."

As the chopper got closer to the target, Robert again spoke to the crew, "Look sharp guys. This LZ is supposed to be secure but we've all heard that before. We could be taking on a lot of ground fire any minute now."

Just then rounds began to hit the chopper. Hank and Alvin began returning fire as fast as their M-60's would fire. They strafed the area below in every direction. This was a hot LZ after all. They were being fired on from all sides. Alvin was shooting from the left side and Hank from the right. Hank yelled to Alvin, "Stay behind your gun for protection, and don't lean out so far."

Alvin yelled back, "You too buddy. This looks like it is going to be hell."

Moments later, things turned for the worse. Robert was hit and killed. His feet came off the foot pedals and the chopper started to circle and drop. Seconds later Dain got hit and was killed. Then Alvin was hit by flying shrapnel. It was all happening so fast. Alvin was thrown over toward Hank who caught him and heard him say, "Thank You Jesus," as he died in his arms.

Falling uncontrollably now, the Huey hit hard. Hank was able to jump out just before it burst into flames. He had also been hit, by small rounds and shrapnel, in the right arm and left chest. He was alive and started crawling for cover in the elephant grass when he tripped a mine and his long journey home began.

The patrol's radio man had seen it all unfold and called in another medevac. The medevac that Hank's crew was initially providing cover for started to pick up the wounded. The medic and crew chief lowered a hoist to retrieve Hank and a couple others. Both watched from the skids making certain the litter they were lowering didn't hit anything as it spun out of control from all the down draft caused by the rotating helicopter blades. Bullets whizzed past their heads and were hitting their chopper as well.

Hank had lost his right leg just below the knee and his left arm just below the elbow when the mine blew. The medic on the ground had placed tourniquets on both extremities. He also thought Hank had a pneumothorax on the left side, and packed a sucking chest wound before putting him on the litter. Hank was lifted up and placed in the chopper along with two other wounded GI's and was flown out to a hospital ship waiting off shore. The ship had been notified to get ready to receive one multi-amputee and two other wounded patients. A usual mission from pick-up to an operating room took about an hour. This one would be less because the medevac chopper was already on the scene and the Hospital Ship REPOSE was just off shore.

Meanwhile, on the REPOSE the loud speaker had barked out, "Flight quarters, flight quarters, now all personnel stand by to receive three emergency litters." Triage personnel reported to duty, the x-ray department was alerted and several operating rooms were placed on alert.

The Navy had two Hospital ships stationed off shore from Vietnam which received battle casualties. The USS REPOSE(AH-16) and the USS SANCTUARY (AH-17). Both resembled the level one trauma centers found in most large cities throughout the United States which specialized in the treatment of severely injured patients. The only exception was that they were floating on water. Both were painted white and had red crosses on their sides. The REPOSE sailed from Da Nang north to the Demilitarized Zone (17th parallel) while the SANCTUARY sailed south from Da Nang.

The REPOSE was a beautiful site to the pilots flying Hank and the others out to her. The medic had been talking to Hank during the entire flight trying to keep him awake so he wouldn't slip in to unconsciousness.

The pilot told the medic to, "Prepare for landing on the helipad." Things had happened so fast. As Hank and the others were off loaded, the medic gave the thumbs up sign to the pilot. He knew that if the wounded were delivered alive they had a 97% survival rate. He then yelled out, "Wind her up. We've got more 'C's to pick up."

Hank was taken to triage, stripped and checked for more wounds. Someone yelled, "Get this guy typed and cross matched for blood." Then he was sent to be x-rayed for shrapnel, bone fragments, bullets. and to see what shape the bones in his right leg and left arm were in. They also found where shrapnel had collapsed his left lung.

He was sent to the operating room where he was prepped for surgery, and an anesthetist put him under for surgery. He spent several hours on the table, while teams of surgeons cleaned and debrided his severed extremities and chest wound. They meticulously removed shrapnel, dirt, wood, and pieces of his uniform out of his wounds.

His left lung was also expanded. Then they closed the open end of his left arm and partially closed the remaining part of his right leg. They applied a pressure dressing on the right stump to help keep the swelling down and improve circulation to the stump. He was taken to the recovery room. His breathing had improved with the lung expansion and he was in serious but stable condition.

In the recovery room, Hank was given large doses of antibiotics and was closely monitored for signs of infection. He made it through the recovery room and was transferred to the intensive care unit until he became more stable. He was then sent to the orthopedic ward where he received daily wound dressing changes. He was constantly monitored for wound infection. When he was well enough, he was transferred to the Army hospital in Da Nang and then to a Continental United States (CONUS) center via Japan. Time was of utmost importance, and getting the wounded on their feet as soon as possible was critical. He couldn't yet recall everything that had happened while the chopper fell to earth. He did recall that the noise was overwhelming as rounds bounced off the chopper's walls. He recalled hearing RPG's exploding and metal being torn apart. He didn't know whether to jump or ride it down. He guested that a blast had apparently blown him out and he landed in the LZ moments before the Huey blew up. He recalled feeling a sharp pain in his left chest and his breathing becoming real labored. The medic told him, "SOB, you tripped a land mine and you're going to beat me home."

While on the REPOSE, Hank asked one of the Red Cross volunteers to get him the addresses of his crew. He wanted to write their families as soon as possible to tell them how proud he was to have served with them. He decided right there and then that he was going to visit each family and let them know how much they had been loved by his buddies. He especially wanted to know why Alvin's last words were," Thank You Jesus". He was on his way stateside to receive convalescent, restorative, and rehabilitative services at one of the Army Amputee Centers, Fitzsimons Army Hospital in Aurora, Colorado.

When the family received word of Hanks injuries, it was heart-breaking. The last time they had seen him was when they dropped him off at boot camp. He was so young and full of life. Now they weren't sure just how they would react when they next saw him. Evenings in the parlor became less of a routine. Hank's grandfather, Bert, didn't seem to care as much about listening to the radio. Listening to baseball games and the news had somehow become less of a priority. Myrtle, his grandmother, had lost a little zip in her step, and his dad would just sit and look more at the paper than reading it. Maybe he was remembering the close call Hank had had when the chainsaw kicked back and cut his leg so badly. He was probably wondering what they would have done if he had lost it that day. Should he now feel sorry for Hank or be glad he was alive? Purvis was trying to make himself helpful around the house, while Janet just cried a lot.

REHABILITATION

Hank eventually arrived at Fitzsimons Army Hospital in Aurora, Colorado. He was fitted with an artificial arm that looked like a hook, along with an artificial leg that was made from plastic and steel. They looked anything but natural. Hank kept thinking at least I have my right arm. He underwent hours of physical therapy(PT) and occupational therapy(OT) and learned to hate every session.

He met other amputees and they shared war stories about how they got injured. They tried to push each other toward a rapid recovery. They laughed and cried together as brothers.

Rick, from Omaha, Nebraska, told them, "I was part of a transportation unit carrying supplies out of Da Nang. We had swept the road for mines on the way out but not on the return trip. It hadn't been that long a trip. Twenty-two of us got burned and I lost my feet when our trucks hit some mines. We were medevac'd out to a hospital ship called the REPOSE and later there was a special medevac to take us to an Army burn unit in Japan. "

Hank interrupted him stating he also had been on the REPOSE. "I just left her a few days ago, after my chopper got shot down. Those medical teams saved my life. I had a collapsed lung and lost my arm and leg, but here I am."

Rick continued, "From Japan, I ended up here. I was lucky to have just lost my feet, several guys died that day. I'm still alive and learning to kick ass again."

Paul was another patient who told them, "I was on patrol when we were ambushed. All hell broke loose and I ended up tripping a damn mine."

They all took time to talk about home, loved ones and the dreams they now had for when they would get out of the military. They tried to encourage each other, especially when one of them would wake up yelling out in fear.

Hank found himself yelling at the staff, "I'm tired of having to have two people put my arm and leg on every morning and take them off at night. I'm tired of being treated like a guinea pig, trying on so many different prosthetics. I don't trust putting my full weight on the damn prosthesis. I can't get over the feeling that my leg is still there, and the pain just doesn't want to go away at times. I feel hopeless. Who will want a cripple like me? I'd rather be dead, like my buddies. Will I ever be able to walk by myself again without help from someone else?"

He asked Sam, another patient, "What pushes you? Why do you put yourself through this day in and day out?"

Sam replied, "I do it so the 'gooks' don't win. I do it for those who didn't come home."

Hank spent the 4th of July in Fitzsimons. He had been injured just weeks earlier and was away from home. The Hospital celebrated the day with a special meal and dignitaries delivering speeches on the importance of the day. Some of the local VFW and American Legion members delivered gifts to the patients and thanked them for their service. This was the first thank you he had heard since arriving in the states. A military band played patriotic selections. All Hank could think of was how he missed not being home and celebrating with his family.

Hank had not been at Fitzsimons long before he noticed the night nurse. She was a pretty girl with brunette hair and dark green eyes. She seemed to have a chip on her shoulder, which puzzled Hank. He started to try and find out what was bothering her.

Catherine had joined the Army shortly after completing nursing school. She joined out of a sense of patriotism instilled by President Kennedy. She had grown up in a working-class Catholic family in

Newark, New Jersey, and was one of five children. Her grandfather had served in the infantry in WW1.

Catherine had completed one tour in Vietnam, 1967 through TET 1968, and had only been at Fitzsimons about five months. Hank wanted to know what it was like being a nurse over there. He learned she had spent six weeks in basic training at Fort Sam Houston before going over to Nam. "While in basic training, I was introduced to a mock Vietnamese village, given M-16 training, and instructions on how to use a compass of all things," she told him. "I'll tell you more tomorrow night. Got to pass some meds now and do some charting."

They met for a short time the next night when he learned some more about her experiences in Nam. "From Ft. Sam, I was sent to the 95th Evacuation Hospital in Da Nang. Some nurses lived in Quonset huts or tents. Some nurses had to share living quarters, while others had private rooms. It was almost impossible to get basic toiletry items. Tampons weren't carried in the Post Exchange (PX) and I had to get my mother to send them, along with tooth paste and shampoo."

She brought some cupcakes the next night and continued her story. It was like she really needed to talk to someone. "Nurses on duty were expected to protect their patients," she continued. She told him stories of nurses putting their own lives at risk protecting their patients. She had heard that at one base, when mortars started hitting it, the nurses dragged patients under their beds and covered them with pillows or, sometimes, with their own bodies.

Hank was becoming more comfortable meeting Catherine during the night shift. It appeared that in his attempt to befriend her, he had opened a Pandora's Box. She started to share more unpleasant memories. "Much of the stress I was under came from the sheer numbers of wounded and disfigured GI's I was assigned to care for. I had to prepare for multiple surgical cases during twelve hour shifts. The casualties came to the hospital in mass from heavily loaded helicopters, both day and night. They forgot to tell us how artillery used in Nam was specifically used to inflict massive, multiple injuries. They didn't tell us about what napalm, white phosphorous, and antipersonnel bombs would do to a person. They didn't prepare us for wounded with burns down to the bone. Not only were we treating wounds, we were treating diseases like typhoid, TB, malaria and bubonic plaque. Sorry, but I have to go now. Duty calls."

On one of the last nights they would meet, Catherine continued. "We were also treating GI's hooked on marijuana, opium, amphetamines, cocaine, and heroin. We might not have received a lot of physical wounds like you guys, but our mental wounds are just as bad. And to think we cannot get any Veterans benefits or join any of the veteran's associations like the VFW or American Legion. We were ill prepared, under trained, unappreciated, sexually harassed, mentally abused, and discriminated against."

Before they ended that last get together, she shared the following story, "One day around Christmas, a General stopped in to hand out some Purple Hearts. All the patients were opening gifts and the mood was real festive. The General went up to one patient who was just opening a gift from home. As he was pinning the medal on, he noticed the gift was a pair of socks, and the patient had no legs. "That, my friend, seems to sum it all up. Vietnam was hell," she added. Catherine thanked Hank for being a sounding board. "It's not often someone notices and cares enough to ask questions. Remember, you did ask what it was like being a nurse in Nam. Remember, a lot of what you are feeling is in your mind. Despite losing your arm and leg, you're still the same valuable person you were before the crash. You will find that as time passes, you will learn to adapt, and your whole attitude will change for the good. The time we spent just talking and listening was helpful. Thanks again, I really needed to vent. I hope we stay in touch."

Hank put in for a transfer. He wanted to get closer to his home in Georgia. Unfortunately for him both Walter Reed, in Maryland,

and Fort Gordon Army Hospital near Augusta, Georgia, were at capacity, so he was sent to the Army's amputee center in Phoenixville, Pennsylvania. When he arrived at Valley Forge Army General Hospital, his mental attitude started to improve.

This new center had several interdisciplinary teams made up of physicians, physical therapist, occupational therapists, nurses, psychologists, psychiatrists, social workers, dieticians and prosthetists. All these members worked together to provide a plan for pain control, emotional support, prevention of skin break down, deconditioning, and muscle loss in the patients they were assigned.

Like Fitzsimons, this facility had amputees in various stages of recovery who offered firsthand accounts of what was expected of him during rehabilitation. "You are going to be on the parallel bars every day. The PT's are going to make sure you leave here walking, and the OT's are going to have you using your left arm like new. There is not going to be any let up, so just get used to it," they told him.

Hank called his family and told them about the move. "This hospital isn't like the last one. The staff seems more laid back and most everyone lives off base. They work shifts like a regular hospital and there's not a lot of military formality. They seem to be interested in not only me physically me but mentally, too. I think I'm going to like it here, and only wish I could have gotten closer to home."

A couple of weeks after his move, the family loaded up the car and headed north to Valley Forge. They wanted to surprise Hank on his birthday. It was going to be a special day and he had no clue they were coming.

When the family arrived at Valley Forge, they found that the hospital was spread out, and consisted of several two-story buildings connected by long ramps. The campus looked more like a college with large trees everywhere, and had over sixty buildings. Hank's ward consisted of several cubicles, each with four beds. Hank was totally taken off guard when his family appeared in the room. He introduced them to his roommates who were playing radios and tape players when they walked in. After a short visit, they took Hank to Philadelphia to celebrate his birthday and take in some of the sites. No one in the family had ever been to Philadelphia and they really wanted to see the Liberty Bell. This had been their first time seeing Hank since he left for boot camp and was injured. He looked pretty good and was getting around without a wheel chair. When they got back to the room, they ate a birthday cake with ice cream, that his buddies had gotten while he was out. It was the best birthday he could have imagined.

The next day, they went out to a local inn, The Buckboard Inn. After lunch, they said their good-byes and headed home. When they arrived back home, Jim told Bert, Myrtle, and Irene, "I think we really surprised him and he enjoyed the visit."

Hank and his new roommates often talked about how they got wounded. Ken, who was from Akron, Ohio, told them, "I lost both my legs when I tripped a mine after going under the wire to call in air strikes."

Tom, from Pittsburg, said, "I lost both my legs when a satchel charge went off at our Fire Base Air Born. Our base was overrun one night in May and we lost a lot of good men and all our artillery guns that night."

Hank said, "I know. I flew on several missions out there. It was up near Hill 937, wasn't it? A damn mess, that one was."

Tom, "Sure was. I heard over 50 of our guys got killed and over 400 were wounded. I also heard over 600 NVA soldiers were killed and no telling how many were buried alive in bunkers and the tunnels our fire base was shelling before it got over run. Our guys took and re-took that damn hill several times before turning it over to the enemy. A lot of good men on both sides died over those 10 days. You know, I never heard how many SVN soldiers died."

Daniel, who was from Atlanta added, "I lost both my hands trying to defuse a bomb. I was on a recon mission and came up on the damn thing. I tried to defuse it, and you see what happened. I'm glad I didn't lose anything else. Damn lucky, I'd say."

At one time or the other they all suffered some form of depression. They played their radios loud during the day and flirted with the nurses, while trying to forget. Many nights they cried themselves to sleep.

Hank took some time off to begin visiting with his crew members families. He told his roommates, "I promised myself to visit all the families and tell them how much each guy loved them and about the crash. I want to let them know how it happened so quickly, and that no one suffered. I especially want to find out from Alvin's family why they thought his last words were 'Thank You Jesus'."

He called Purvis and Alvin's dad, Buck, to set up a visit. Purvis was able to rent a Ford Econoline van to take them to Dothan, Alabama. He picked up Hank and they headed south.

When Hank finally met Alvin's family, he learned a lot about his buddy. He met his mother, Mable, who was a seamstress and worked from home. Prom-dresses, Easter dresses and wedding dresses were her specialty. She told Hank, "Alvin had grown up with a chip on his shoulders. He knew he was from the wrong side of the tracks. He had little education, no job experience and no one would hire him. Alvin was headed down a one-way street until he got drafted. Oh, I tried to raise him proper, you know. I took him to church every Sunday and all that. I hoped the Army would be good for him, and was proud to tell my Sunday school class about all he was doing."

"I always thought Alvin was living in his own personal hell on earth, at times, despite all my efforts to keep him straight. I know he had accepted the Lord and felt some comfort knowing that if anything happened to him over there, he'd be ok."

Alvin's dad was a mechanic for a local car dealership. He, like Mable, was active in the local AME church where he was a Deacon and taught Sunday school. He told Hank, "It was difficult trying to keep a young teenager straight with so much segregation, you know. I hoped that one day I could open my own garage and he'd join me."

"The Army seemed to change all that. Vietnam seemed to change him. He wrote us often about how he'd been accepted from the beginning of boot camp right through Nam. He wrote us about Robert, Dain and you and how y'all treated him the same. How much you depended on each other and that y'all didn't see color, you saw a brother. Thanks for being so good to him."

Hank, "Don't thank me, it was easy. We were brothers. You know he was always telling us he missed his mother's cooking. 'Mom could really cook up a spread; ham, potato salad, coleslaw, and fresh baked biscuits that would melt in your mouth'," he'd say.

"He wrote us saying he was seriously considering staying in the Army. He kind of wanted to become a crew chief like Dain and Danny. He told us Danny's dad was also a mechanic and owned his own shop. He even thought about moving up the ranks like Dain and getting his own wings."

Hank added, "I remember Dain talking to Alvin about his time at Fort Wolters, Texas, and his advanced training at Fort Rucker, in Alabama. He told him at Wolters they went through two "spit-and-polished" boot camps. The preflight school for WOC's like himself was four weeks of hell. If your socks or uniforms were not in order, you could bring down fire on the entire class. The more you cleaned, the more they looked. They were teaching us to remain cool and steady under constant pressure. 'If you can't take this, you can't take combat either,' the training officers kept repeating. The first part of the day was spent learning how to hover and the second part was learning how to be an officer, the Army way."

"At Fort Rucker, we learned instrument flight rules, tactics, formation flying, and how to fly the Huey," I heard him tell Alvin.

Hank continued, "I think in his own way Dain was trying to discourage Alvin. The war was getting worse, and if he had a chance to get home and work with you, that sounded pretty good to Dain."

Buck answered, "I wish he'd been able to stay in or at least come home and join me at the garage. Man, I sure do miss that kid."

Hank replied, "I do too. Let's go out and see that panel. I can't begin to tell you how many hours we spent talking about modifications he wanted to do to it when he got back ". They went out and cranked the panel up. It looked sort of plain and needed work. Buck said, "Don't worry I'm going to finish her up like Alvin wrote me, so he'll be proud."

Hank left the family realizing that Alvin had been brought up in a spiritual family and that he had accepted the Lord at a young age. He knew he was with his brothers Robert and Dain. It wasn't until he was half way back to Valley Forge that he realized he'd failed to ask Alvin's family why he might have been thanking Jesus at the end.

He knew it wouldn't be long after he got back to the hospital that a medical board would discharge him from active service and he'd be transferred to a VA Prosthetic facility. There, he would be treated as an inpatient under retired status. This would allow for continued rehabilitation along with more prosthetic fittings. He figured he might even have to get a job to live on.

He started to get scared about being on his own. The possibility of not being able to find a job reminded him of Alvin and how nobody wanted to hire him. He called Purvis to share his concerns.

"Who wants to hire a disabled person?", he asked. "I've already sent out a few feelers and heard nothing. Heck, I can't even get an interview. When I do get to see someone, all they see is a cripple. Who wants to hire a guy with only one leg and one arm? I can't even lift fifty pounds or stand on my feet for long periods of time. I only have a high school education and no real work history other than the Army. There are so many able-bodied Vets returning home, I don't have a chance. Who wants a crippled 'baby-killer'?"

Purvis answered, "The only thing I can think of is, don't give up, try harder. You can always come home, we have plenty of work for you. I've been doing pretty well with only one good hand. You were handling things pretty good when we went to Dothan. You've made a lot of progress. Keep positive and don't let them win."

Hank thought about Purvis last words, "Don't let them win." He was doing better. He could put on his hook arm and leg without assistance. He had learned to walk straight and tie his shoes. He was learning how to drive. He could get in the car and put it in gear, and was driving pretty good now. He could open a jar and tie a tie. Yes, he was doing pretty good after all.

He continued, for a while, to stay up beat, but after a new batch of patients came in and shared their stories, he began to relive that fateful day when he was shot down. He decided to call Purvis and see if he would rent another van, or maybe a car this time, and go see Robert's family in Rochester, Minnesota.

Kelly met them at the door. She was as beautiful as Robert had described her. Robert's daughters, Heather and Jennifer, were also lovely. Heather now 13 and Jennifer was 10. They greeted Hank with open arms. Robert would have been so proud of them. It became apparent early on that they missed their dad very much.

Kelly sensed how much it pained Hank to speak about Robert and told him, "Several of Roberts letters spoke so highly of your friendship. He wrote about all his crew. He was excited about Dain becoming a Warrant Officer and flying with him. He told us Alvin wanted to stay in the military and make something of himself. Other times, he wrote about the difficulty Alvin must have been going through trying to choose between the service and going home to work with his dad. They were going to rebuild a truck or something, weren't they?"

Hank, "Yeah, a '53 Chey panel truck. I saw it when I visited Alvin's family not long ago. His dad is still going to complete it as a tribute to Alvin and the crew."

Kelly continued, "He even talked about you being from Willacoochee, Georgia. I had to look it up on the map. Do you really kill a pig on the Fourth of July and cook it slowly over wood coals all night long?"

"Yes ma'am. Y 'all will have to come down and join us one year. There's a lot to do on the Fourth and we have plenty of room for you. Remember to take your sun tan lotion and shorts, because it should be hot."

"What's this I hear about you skinny dipping on moonless nights?" she asked.

Hank said, "He really didn't tell you about that, did he?" Kelly laughed as his face started turning red.

Kelly, "Well, tell me what you are going to do with yourself now that you're going to be getting out of the Army."

This threw Hank, for some reason. The way she asked the question, it was like he didn't have a disability. She didn't see him as a cripple. He answered, "I'm thinking of how I'm going to get a job and keep one. I want to work with the vets, I think."

The conversation shifted back to Robert and some of the missions he flew. He told the girls how their dad flew VIP's during Bob Hope's Christmas show in 1968. He told them about a medevac mission where his chopper got all shot up.

"He knew better than to write us about that one," Kelly chimed in. "We were worry warts as it was."

Hank continued, "He told us how he would go ice fishing every winter, and how he would cut a hole in the pond ice and fish through it. Said he'd catch more beers than fish. We learned a lot about each other during down time and became true brothers. He couldn't stop talking about y'all."

"He told us how proud he was of you girls and how much he loved you. He said that Jennifer was in the fourth grade and was as smart and beautiful as her mom. He said you could do anything you wanted and bragged about how smart you were. He said you were a cheerleader and could serve a mean tennis ball.

"He would say that Heather is in the seventh grade and enjoys music and golf. He was looking forward to hearing you playing in a high school band one day at football games. Or watching you tee it up in a tournament one day. 'She is always hitting practice shots.'"

Before they left for the cemetery Kelly handed Hank a letter, "This arrived with Robert's personal effects. It is a letter from his dad."

"Dear Son, I am sorry I have not written sooner. There just is not a lot of news at this end. I am glad you have started coloring in the days on the girly calendar. Won't be long now. I am sure you are staying up on local events through the girls and nationally listening to the Armed Forces Radio along with reading the Stars and Stripes. The Twins are having a pretty good year. Looks like Martin has put together a good roster and Killebrew is having a good season so far. Maybe they will end up playing Baltimore for the ALCS.

"Mother and I are proud of what you are doing. Don't listen to all the demonstration talk. Those of us who know what is going on over there are real proud of the job you are doing. May your days be clear with a light tail wind. Love, Dad."

Kelly said, "I'm thinking about getting this framed for the girls."

As the day came to a close, they went out to the cemetery. There, Hank took Kelly to the side and told her, "Call me anytime you need anything. Robert was a fine person, husband, officer, and brother. I was proud to have known him and you can be proud of his service and love for his family. There are times I wish I hadn't survived the crash, because I miss him so much. He went quickly and I'm certain he didn't feel any pain. His last words to the crew were, 'Look sharp guys. We could be taking on a lot of ground fire any minute now.' He was always thinking about us."

They all hugged, kissed and promised to always stay in touch. Purvis and Hank got in the car and headed back to Valley Forge.

Hank felt good about the trip and called home and told his family, "It was important for them to know how much Robert loved them and about his service to our country. This visit has given me new motivation to continue to become more independent and make something of myself. I want to live for the guys", he added.

His mother responded, "I'm proud of you for going to visit them and can't wait for Purvis to get safely home. I'm sure he will have more to tell us about the trip. Take care son, we love you."

HOMEWARD BOUND

Augusta, Georgia, is known for its major golf tournament, a nearby nuclear bomb plant, Fort Gordon, and the Medical College of Georgia. It is located on the banks of the Savannah River which separated South Carolina and Georgia. More importantly, it was only three and a half hours from Willacoochee, Georgia, Hank's home. Hank was going to the Augusta VA for rehabilitation and more prosthetic fittings.

Hank called his parents when he got settled in and told them that the hospital was eight stories tall, painted white and sat on the top of the highest point in Augusta. "It used to be a hotel where all the rich tourists from up north came to play golf in the winter. In addition to this golf course, there are several more in the area. It must have been spectacular in it's heyday. He continued, "I arrived just a few days after some sort of riot here. You might have seen it on the news or heard about it on the radio. I believe some boy was found dead in the jail, and all heck broke loose. The local TV says six people have been killed, with sixty-people injured and several others still missing. James Brown, a nationally recognized singer and hometown celebrity, flew in to help settle things down. All this excitement reminded me about what Alvin must have gone through living with segregation in Dothan, Alabama."

Hank started to relive the crash and all that had happened that day. He thought he was getting over all that, but realized he wasn't. After all, the doctors were telling him it was just depression or battle fatigue he was experiencing. They just kept prescribing pills.

He kept waking up at night, sweating, hearing Alvin's last words, 'Thank You Jesus.'

He became a short fuse and started yelling at people for no apparent reason. "Why did they die and I lived?" he would keep asking the nurses. They had no answers for him and just held his hand and listened. He called home and told his mother what was happening. She could only answer, "Only God knows, son. Calm down and listen to Him. He will give you direction." After the call, his family decided to drive up to Augusta and pay him a visit.

When they got to Augusta, they drove up a massive brick driveway leading to the hospital. They now knew where a lot of the sand from the Alapaha River, which their grandfather shipped, ended up. The driveway was shaded by tall magnolia trees and there was a large central grassed area. The hospital was a lot bigger than Valley Forge and was connected to other treatment areas by a maze of outside wooden corridors, which had been added when it became a hospital.

Hank was in one of the wings and seemed to really perk up when he saw the family. It was a pretty day so he suggested they go for a walk around the hospital and see the grounds. He wanted to show off just how much he had improved since their last visit at Valley Forge.

He told Purvis, "I can handle my loss of limbs pretty well now. My strength is good and my balance great. It's the little things that still frustrate me, like how to scratch an itch, how to push the tooth paste out of the tube, how to get these damn underpants on, or put soap on a washcloth."

Purvis said, "You'll get back to normal soon enough. Thank goodness you didn't lose your dominant right arm."

Hank said, "Yeah, at least I can shake somebody's hand and look them straight in the eye. A strong handshake means a lot, you know. The staff keeps telling me I might enjoy playing golf one day. Imagine me playing golf! They have a good course right here on the campus where plenty of the handicapped patients play for exercise. Who knows, maybe I'll try it."

The family took Hank out for lunch before heading back home. Hank's mother told him, "Everything is going to be all right. Maybe you'll meet someone new here or get released soon. We all miss you at home so much. I'm proud of you son".

Janet answered, "I love you so much and miss you. See you at home soon."

His father added, "It won't be long now before you're home. Take care of yourself."

Purvis could only add, "Later, bro."

Hank met a vet named Ron in the lounge area one morning. Ron had been a sergeant in Nam and was waiting on some prescriptions. As they talked, Ron began to tell some stories from his time over there.

"I grew up in Evansville, Indiana. It, like Augusta is to Georgia, is the second largest city in Indiana. I enlisted in the Army in 1968 after graduation from Indiana State University. I went through basic training at Fort Campbell, Kentucky, making $91.00 a month. After basic training, I was sent to Fort Lee, Virginia. "

"I arrived in Nam in January under a red flag alert at Long Binh. The next day, I was at an outpost called Don Binh Than, which is about half way between Phan Rangh and Nu Trang on Highway 1. It's across the bay from Cam Ranh Bay. The Airforce had a huge base at Cam Ranh. It had toilets, street lights, paved streets; California personified,"

They decided to go to the cafeteria for lunch where Ron continued his memories. "Sally was a year behind me in high school, age wise. I was fairly good at tennis, number 3 or 4 on my high school's tennis team. Sally and I challenged each other several times. She beat me every time.

"One morning I was on a LZ when I heard the Whop-whop of helicopter blades. I was told it was the 'Donut Dollies'. And, hey,

I like donuts. I was surprised, amazed, to see Sally jump off that Huey! Small world.

"Sally later told me that she graduated from college and decided to join the Red Cross and become a 'Donut Dolly' in Vietnam. She said that she remembered President Kennedy saying, "Ask not what your country can do for you, but what you can do for your country. 'I came armed with one mission, that of morale booster for all the troops.'

"It wasn't a new idea, there were 'Donut Dollies' in WWII and they traveled in clubmobiles (converted buses), visiting the troops. They were in Korea and now here. 'We fly everywhere to give the GI's a taste of home. It makes the world seem a little smaller for the guys, even if it's just for a day.'

"We had bad times too," Ron continued. "Our roommate, Gary, was on guard duty one night when we had a sapper attack. He was wounded in the chest, but took out two VC. He received a Bronze Star and a Purple Heart.

"Another sapper attack that woke up our village was when a huge water buffalo stumbled into our concertina wires, rattled the tin cans, and set off a full alert. Talk about the rockets red flares; the bombs bursting in air. There was no night thanks to the hundreds of flares going off. The M-60's were off. The M-16's were afire. Needless to say, that buffalo made the biggest mistake of his life. We had steak for the next three days."

A little later Ron recalled how Jeannie, his wife, and he met in Hawaii for his R&R in late 1969. "We decided to visit the Arizona Memorial one day. We rented a car and drove to the Memorial. It was late and the gates were closed; locked shut. She surmised the Arizona was out on maneuvers. I've never figured out to this day if she was kidding or not."

Ron went on to tell several more stories as the days passed. One story was about when he left Nam, "My last night in Vietnam was, thank God, uneventful. I reported to Cam Ranh Bay the next morning to board my freedom bird which took off about ten P.M. I noticed that there were about 10 seats vacant on the 747. I didn't wonder why. I shuddered to think why?"

"When we finally took off south, the pilot banked and headed north to Osaka, Japan. He came on the speaker and said, 'Welcome aboard, to you heroes. Our flight to Japan is six hours, twelve hours to Anchorage and another four hours to Seattle. As we turn and head back toward Cam Ranh Bay I'm going to dim the cabin lights so you folks can have a final look.' To the man there were 200+ BOOS!!!!!."

Ron and Hank had some great visits and it helped them both to talk over their memories. The more stories they shared, the more comfortable they became dealing with all the traumatic experiences they had gone through.

While Hank lay in bed one night, he started to think of all the ways those who served in Vietnam returned home. Most, like Ron, flew home on the 'Freedom Bird'. It was a regular civilian jet with beautiful stewardesses. These were usually the first women the guys had seen in months. The flight home was much more jovial than the flight over. He remembered how excited Robert had been when he was a short timer. "Won't be long before I'm boarding the 'Freedom Bird' and heading home," he had told them.

Some of the GI's flew home in transport planes. They weren't quite as fancy as the 'Freedom Bird', but that didn't stop the excitement from those who boarded them. "I finally made it out of this hell hole," was the phrase most heard at takeoff. It was much better taking off headed east than west.

Others returned on the same ships that had carried them over. These were the carriers, transport vessels, cruisers, destroyers, replenishment ships, and hospital ships that helped keep the war moving.

He thought of the thousands going home to loved ones in caskets draped by the American Flag. They were carried by honor guards to homes across the States, after paying the ultimate price by giving their lives.

Hank also thought about the veterans who still haven't made it home. The MIA's and POW's from all wars whose families are hoping and praying their loved ones will soon complete their long journey.

 Last, but not least, are the souls lying in the Tomb of the Unknown Soldier. The Tomb is the final resting place for Unknowns from WWI, WWII and the Korean War, and is guarded at all times.

Hank met a Hospital Corpsman name Scott who had served in Nam. He was in front of him in the cafeteria line one day and Hank heard him tell the guy in front that he'd been in Nam '69-'70. Hank invited him to his table and they hit it off right away. Hank asked Scott; "How did you come home?" Scott was more than willing to share his journey home. "I was stationed on the hospital ship USS REPOSE. She was one of the two hospital ships the Navy had in Nam. The other ship was The USS SANCTUARY and both sailed in the combat waters off the shore of Nam receiving wounded via helicopters.

"The war was just starting to downsize the troops in the early 70's shortly after the '69 TET offensive. The REPOSE had served proudly during her tour and was selected to be decom- missioned effective March 1970. I had been on board about ten months at that time. We all received a REPOSE Year Book 1969-1970 and a Departure Ceremony Pamphlet dated March 14, 1970.

"In the Departure Ceremony Pamphlet, I remembered reading that from February 1966 when the REPOSE arrived in Vietnam, through March 1970, more than 24,000 patients had been admitted for in-patient care. More than 9,000 were battle casualties. Besides American service and civilian personnel, those treated included Vietnamese civilians, Thai, Filipino, Chinese, Korean, and French personnel, to mention just a few.

"From Vietnam, the REPOSE sailed to the Philippines, Hong Kong, Japan, Hawaii and on to Oakland, California. I remember sailing under the Golden Gate Bridge in San Francisco. I won't ever forget seeing the cliffs on the California coast."

Hank interrupted, "I was taken to the REPOSE, after my Huey gunship was shot down. My buddies were killed, but I managed to get out somehow before it crashed and burned. I tripped a mine going for cover in razor sharp elephant grass and got messed up pretty bad. The crew on the REPOSE did a great job keeping me alive."

At lunch the next day, Hank learned that Scott had recently started as an orderly on one of the medical units. Scott was glad to have met someone he could relate to, and he told Hank about a trip he and some buddies took when they were in the Philippines. "We took a bus, from Subic Bay to Manila, which is the capital of the Philippines. The bus was boarded by some local militia and we didn't know what to do. The militia men looked real rough and they were carrying rifles. They walked through the hot, dusty bus looking for rebels, most likely. What they found was a bus full of Philippine natives carrying goods to markets in Manila and let us pass. Most of the passengers were elderly women staring quietly out open windows. Many of them were probably my age when WWII invaded their pristine islands. The women looked tired, expressionless, and had wrinkled, thick dry skin which resembled leather. Many were carrying baskets full of vegetables, eggs, chickens, and other goods to market. As we traveled the dusty dirt road on to Manila, we saw a John Deere tractor plowing a nearby field."

Scott was on a roll. The next day he continued the story. He recalled, "Manila was in marked contrast to the impoverished country side we had just travelled through. It was, by all standards, a most modern city rivalling those found stateside. We checked into an internationally known hotel that was just as modern as any hotel found in the states. It had the biggest chandelier we had ever seen hanging in the lobby. Our rooms were clean and had all the creature comforts of home including TV and thick white bath towels.

"I remember seeing jeepneys everywhere. They were the most popular means of public transportation at the time. The 'Philippine Jeepneys' were famous tourist attractions and were packed full of tourist and locals hanging off of them. You see, they were made from jeeps left after the war and were brightly colored with birds and flowers. They remined me of the bus seen in the Partridge Family TV show."

Scott invited Hank over to his apartment to meet his roommate Jonathan. Jonathan worked as a paralegal for a law firm. During supper, Scott continued to tell about his journey home. Jonathan had never heard it and listened intently. "The ship sailed from Subic Bay, in the Philippines, to Hong Kong where it stayed for two weeks in a real big harbor that was surrounded by mountains. Hong Kong was a beautiful site by night with all the buildings lit up, reflecting on the water. During the daytime, it took on an entirely different appearance, as poverty was seen everywhere. People were sleeping, cooking and living in the gutters. Clothes were hanging between buildings. People were sitting in windows trying to keep cool. Then you'd see 'Junk Boats' everywhere, traveling between ships picking up left overs tossed overboard by the crews. Entire families lived on these once valued boats that had carried cargo inland years before and helped a growing China. The families ate, slept and raised animals on these boats which are now falling into disrepair.

"After Hong Kong, the ship sailed to Osaka, Japan, where I went to see Expo '70. The Exposition was a great way for countries to show off their progress in science and technology. At each stop I was greeted like a hero, especially while visiting Expo '70 where everyone bowed and wanted a picture beside me in my uniform.

"We left Japan and arrived in Pearl Harbor to a Navy band playing for us. The USO even threw a traditional luau and made us feel welcomed.

"After Hawaii, we sailed to San Francisco and in to Oakland, California. I didn't know there were cliffs on the coast there, and I was speechless as we sailed under the Golden Gate Bridge. In Oakland, I was told to take my uniform off before heading home. In the states, Vietnam wasn't very popular and those returning were considered 'Baby-Killers'.

"You know, it's funny in a way that the same guy that had a leg fall off in his hands while trying to save a soldier could, at the same time, be called a 'baby-killer'. People in the states just didn't get it. I was proud to be a Corpsman and proud of all those I served with during my time aboard the REPOSE. Hooyah!"

A while later, Hank did meet a new Occupational therapist. Her name was Marie and she was from middle Georgia, down near Swainsboro. She had trained at the Medical College of Georgia and had hired on at the VA. She was slender with brown hair and the deepest brown eyes you could imagine. She had a great smile and the personality to go along with it. She didn't take crap off anyone and could dish it out just as good as many of the guys under her care. When Hank was down, she'd make him feel silly by reminding him just how good he had it. "Heck sake, most of the men who had your injuries never made it home." Her constant attention and pushing him, along with her constant encouragement, were starting to grow on him. He found himself daydreaming of a possible relationship.

He had to call his mother to tell her about Marie. "She's the most beautiful girl I've ever met. She knows how to relate to me, and really listens to me. She understands what I'm going through and knows when to say something or not. She seems to know me better than anyone I've ever met. I just don't know if she feels the same about me, or if she's just doing her job."

Hank's mother suggested he should start spending more time with her outside of the therapy room. She even suggested they meet for lunch or something. "Ask God to direct you," she added.

Hank found himself coming up with reasons to see her outside of the treatment room. He asked her to lunch in the cafeteria and she agreed to meet him. The lunches became more frequent and they started to meet after her shift was over. They would walk around the campus or just sit and talk.

Hank told her about Robert, Dain and Alvin, and told her how they died. He shared things with her about himself, and that he wanted to accomplish all the goals she had set for him. He called Purvis to tell him all this and how happy he was. Purvis told him, "You should go for it, she sounds like the perfect girl for you. Just don't talk about the war. Tell her something about yourself. Be cool and keep things upbeat."

Hank started thinking of how he would ever be able to provide for Marie. He only had his disability compensation. Maybe if he went to college, he could get the GI Bill.

He often dreamed about how she would react to being held by a man with only one arm. Could she ever imagine lying beside a man with only one arm and one leg? Could he ever be able to satisfy her sexually? He couldn't get her out of his mind. He told Purvis," She knows just where to touch me, how to look at me and when to distance herself from me. It's kind of spooky in a way."

Purvis could only say, "Sounds serious, bro. Things are moving pretty fast, it sounds like. Don't go and get cold feet now, go for it. I want to meet her. She sounds like a great girl."

Hank did start to get cold feet. He got scared and put in for a transfer to the Dublin VA. He told Marie he wanted to get closer to home. He kept telling himself that if it was to be, then things would work out. His decision seemed to really upset Marie at first until she realized he needed to be closer to home and they really had not known each other very long.

Hank decided to look for a place of his own near Dublin, Georgia, and the VA. He was able to get a used car, and to rent some property near Adrian, which was located about halfway between

Dublin and Swainsboro. He had decided to go to college at East Georgia College in Swainsboro, and combined his GI Bill, and disability pay to make an offer on the Adrian property. He told Marie about it and she seemed really excited for him. She said, "I'll see you in a couple of weeks when I visit Mom and Dad. They live just outside of Swainsboro."

The house he rented was built in two sections with a breezeway connecting them and a high-pitched tin roof covering the entire house and surrounding porch. The locals referred to houses built like this as 'Dogtrots'. Both sections were open floor plans and identical in size, about 20'x24'. One side served as the parlor, bedroom and bath. The other side was used for the kitchen, dining room, guest room, and had a small bathroom. There were a couple of old church pews in the breezeway. Hank used one to sit on when he removed his work clothes.

The house was made of wood and sat on 2.5 acres of land, with an option to buy up to 10 more acres. There was an old outhouse downwind from the house which had a half-moon cutout in the door. It must have been the home of a family working on what was once a plantation, because there were several more such structures scattered around the area.

Hank took a weekend and went to see his family. He told them about Marie, "She's the most beautiful person I've ever met. She seems to know me so well and wants to learn more about me. I want to make something of myself so that one day I'll be able to support her. I want you all to meet her. Maybe when she comes down to see her family she can meet you."

Hank had one more trip to make before he could get further involved. He and Purvis decided to make the final trip to Lubbock, Texas, and see Dain's family. He called Dain's wife, Barbara, and set the date.

They took his car and headed for Lubbock during a quarter break at college. When they arrived, they soon learned what was meant about Texas hospitality. Barbara met them with open arms. Hank had gone out there to lift her spirits and she was lifting his. She had olive colored skin, dark hair and deep dark eyes. She had a big Texas smile. Barbara taught special education at a local middle school. "We almost decided to have a child when Dain came home for pilot training at Wolters. But knowing he would be going back over put a stop to that idea. He learned that, at onetime Wolters was sending 300 pilots a month to Nam. He didn't want to leave me pregnant, in case something happened."

Dain's mother and dad drove over from Plainview, Texas, to meet him. Plainview was about an hour drive north of Lubbock. Mr. Jacobs was a salesman for a meat processing plant there and his wife, Catherine, was a secretary for a law practice.

Hank mentioned, "It sure is flat land out here. Dain used to tell us how flat the countryside was, and that when he flew to Wolters he could see the water tower in Plainview just after takeoff. The tower was in plain view pardon the pun, some forty miles north."

"He was right. That water tower is about forty miles away," Mr. Jacobs said. "We'd go out west of town on highway 70, towards Muleshoe, to watch thunderstorms and twisters nearly thirty miles away. We can see them coming long before any warning sirens go off in town. There are no trees or pollution to block your view, and there's no prettier sight than to see lightening dancing in the tops of huge thunderheads."

Hank told them, "Dain and I would spend many an hour trying to convince each other which state produced the most cotton, Texas or Georgia. He always said it was Texas because the Lubbock area alone produced more cotton than Georgia. Alvin thought Alabama produced a lot of cotton. "Bet, it's Alabama," he'd say."

Dain's mother and father told him, "We were mighty proud of Dain when he got his wings. He shared so many stories with us about Nam, and how proud he was to be a crew member with y'all. We only wish he had given us a grandchild."

Hank tried to liven up the visit by telling them how Dain tried to convince us there were UFO's out there because lights had been seen over Lubbock in the early fifties. His parents just laughed and said, "Sure enough, the papers were full of sightings. Funny thing though, we haven't heard of any since."

Hank went on about how much they looked forward to Barbara's care packages. "We'd put Texas Pete on everything because the Army chow wasn't that great. Texas Pete on scrambled eggs with sausages and biscuits never tasted so good."

By the end of the visit, Hank was glad he'd made the trip. He told them, "I was so proud to have served with Dain. He was a fine person, a great officer, and a true hero. He helped save many lives during his time in Nam, and I will be forever grateful to have known him." Purvis and he headed home after a short visit to the cemetery.

Back in Georgia, Marie had managed to get a transfer to the Dublin VA. They would be together again. Hank couldn't get her out of his head. They began seeing each other regularly and she made several trips to Adrian. Then one day, under the live oaks that are found on the campus of the VA, Hank asked her to marry him. Marie answered, "I thought you'd never ask me. Why do you think I transferred here? Did you think I moved here just because you were a good guy? Sure, I'll marry you. Even if you are a big lug!" They called their parents with the good news and started to make plans.

Hank spent his first Veterans Day in his new home. He and Marie drove over to the VA Hospital to attend several of the events scheduled for the day. They visited some patients and enjoyed the cookout provided by the hospital. The cookout was held on the grounds of the hospital under the sprawling live oaks. Hank had a new appreciation for what the day meant for the veterans because of all the sacrifices they had made.

By this time, Hank was taking classes at East Georgia. He was on his way to becoming a mental health professional. This was something he had been thinking of as a career ever since reading about how they were helping vets who were suffering from battle fatigue/depression. Veterans like himself weren't getting a lot of help from psychiatrists and psychologists at the VA centers because most of them had never been in combat. They had no clue what some of their patients had been through.

Hank told Purvis, "Most of them don't have any idea what it is like to go to bed with a M-16 at your side. Or what it meant to fly on dangerous missions, with the enemy shooting at you, much less seeing people die. They can't begin to understand what it means to have a brother die in their arms. All they want to do is prescribe medication, anxiety pills, antidepressants, and stuff like that. I don't think they really want to feel what you're feeling. 'Just take two of these pills so you'll feel ok, and follow up with me in a couple of months,' is their standard answer for everybody."

Thanksgiving Day was spent with Marie's family, enjoying a traditional meal of turkey, stuffing, mashed potatoes with gravy, cranberry sauce, and biscuits. After they had eaten way too much, Marie and her mom spent the better part of the day talking about the fast approaching wedding while Jim and Hank took a nap.

The next morning Hank drove to Willacoochee. While traveling he remembered what the nurse at Fitzsimons, Catherine, had told him about her service. He later told Purvis what she had said about not all the women in Vietnam were 'Donut dollies', 'chopper chicks' or 'Kool-Aid kids'. She said, "Most of us were over there on a mission that involved treating our GI's wounds. If the men are finding it hard getting help for their trauma disorders, think how hard it is for the women. Many of us have been cut off from even the most traditional channels for help and are being completely ignored. We can't even speak out about how we were treated when we came home, or how we couldn't join service organizations like the VFW. We were ineligible for government compensation or benefits like counseling". Hank told Purvis, "I want to help people like Catherine who aren't getting much help from anybody, even if it's just listening to them, because she had seen man's inhumanity to man in the wounds she cared for and now in a nation which was so full of anger."

He told Purvis, "Marie makes me feel so special, because she knows how to listen to me and doesn't put a lot of time restraints on me. She seems to know just how much Robert and the guys meant to me and how much we laughed together and depended on each other. They were my brothers. But you know, there's something still missing. I just can't put my finger on it. This should be a festive time of the year, but I'm just not feeling it."

Hank told his family, "Everything is happening so fast. It doesn't seem that long ago that I joined the Army, went to boot camp, flew to Nam, and got shot down. Now I'm about to marry Marie and I'm getting scared. I just can't believe she really loves me that much." His mother tried to reassure him, "It will be ok, she knows exactly what she's getting into." Despite all the reassurances, Hank began to get have second thoughts.

He told his dad, "I keep thinking about Marie, and if I will ever be able to provide for her in the ways I want too. Hell, I can't even find a job right now."

Jim answered back, "I thought the same as you when I asked your mother to marry me. How was I going to provide for her on a pulp-wood salary? Don't forget you have a lot of benefits which I never had. You have the GI Bill, a disability package, and soon her salary. You have a lot to be thankful for, and should be set for the rest of your life."

Hank later told Purvis, "Oh, she acts like I'm able to satisfy her sexually, but I just keep thinking she's faking it. I can get aroused ok, but I don't know if I'm completely satisfying her."

Purvis said, "I don't know if any man really has an answer for that. Just go with the flow, or ask her."

"Yeah, but by the time I get my hook and leg off, the mood is usually long gone. We have to be ready early in the mornings or late at night when I'm not all hooked up."

Purvis could only sympathize with him but added, "Sounds like you are the one with the problem. Has she complained? I'm sure she's thought about it, too, and still wants to be your wife. It will all work out."

With most of his new fears addressed, Hank felt better about getting married. The big day came and they married at her family church in Swainsboro, where she had been baptized. The church had the most beautiful stained-glass windows, and sat a couple hundred worshippers.

Marie's dad gave her away, and Jim was Hank's best man. Janet was a bridesmaid and Purvis one of the groomsmen. Buck and his wife came over from Dothan and were treated like family. Marie was dressed in a gorgeous white gown and Hank was in a tux. It turned out to be the hottest mid-December day on record so far and the air conditioner was wide open. Hank later told one of his buddies at the VA, "I couldn't stop sweating. The preacher handed me a towel to dry my forehead off with when I was kneeling at the altar. I couldn't help wandering if this was some kind of sign for what lay ahead. I was so embarrassed."

NEW BEGINNING

The marriage started off great. There was the usual excitement and expectation like all newly- weds experience. Hank's goals were to complete two years at East Georgia and then to transfer to Georgia Southern in Statesboro. He wanted to get a degree in psychology. He told Marie, "I want to start a horse therapy program when I graduate. We don't need pills, we need nonjudgmental care." Marie agreed and told him, "I'm all in. I love you so much."

Marie was having a great time working but was concerned about Hank driving so much, back and forth to college. Everything was going along good except for that. It had been almost twelve months now since the crash. Hank had been able to keep his promise and had visited his crew's families. He had a new wife, a new home with some land, and was going to college. He had ambitious goals and never questioned what could go wrong? As the anniversary of the crash drew near, Hank started waking up in cold sweats and yelling out. Marie would comfort him by holding him, rocking him, and saying, "It's going to be ok." She began to walk around the house on pins and needles, not wanting to upset him. She told her folks, "He keeps waking up, reliving the crash and seeing his buddies dying. He yells out, 'Why did I survive?' It's really beginning to worry me." Her mother said, "Why don't y'all start coming over here after church? Maybe he just needs to get around other people and relax."

Marie's dad, Al, was a tall, striking, self-made farmer, who also served as a county commissioner. He owned several hundred acres of land, mostly producing cotton and soybeans. Hank was overwhelmed by the amount of property Marie's family owned and began saying things like, "I will never be able to provide for you the way your family provided for you." She answered, "I am not interested in that or things. I've got you and that's all I want."

One day, seemingly out of nowhere, Hank told Marie, "I think we need to separate for a couple of months and see what happens. College isn't working out. I'm tired of all the driving and carrying all those damn books. I'm tired of people looking at me like I'm a freak and calling me a 'Baby killer' behind my back. I'm tired of being treated like a second- class citizen and hearing people saying that's why they objected to the war. I'm tired of thinking you want more from me than I can give. I'm just tired right now. Heck sake, I don't even think your dad really likes me. I guess I'm not the perfect son-in-law he imagined for you." Marie was taken completely off guard for the first time, and could not think of anything to say except, "If that's the way you feel, then let's try it for a couple of months."

Hank called his family with the news, "Marie and I are going to separate for a while. She's going to move in with her family and I'm staying here. I'm dropping out of college and going to try and get my head screwed back on." Both his mother and dad couldn't really say much, other than," See you soon. We love you." They were in a state of shock.

Marie confronted her dad one evening. She came straight out and asked him, "Do you like Hank? He has this feeling that you don't, and thinks you believe he's not good enough for me. He thinks it's because he can't get a job, that he dropped out of college, and is a cripple."

Her dad was taken off guard by Marie's question and comments. He could only respond, saying, "I never even thought of him that way. He's a pretty good kid. I just hope he can make you happy. I am concerned that if he loves you, then why did he suggest this separation?"

"He left to get his head screwed back on. It wasn't that long ago that he was shot down and lost all his buddies. Dad, I'm proud of him. He joined the military when others were fleeing to Canada, and protesting the war. He fought for our freedom and received several wounds. He has goals, but he keeps hitting obstacles everywhere he turns. Hank really wants to do right by me and is just looking for a break. He came back here, bought a home, and is trying to start a horse therapy program to help his fellow vets. He's good to me and he loves me. I'm hanging in there with him, no matter what. After all, I married him, not you."

During the next month, Hank continued to visit the VA as an outpatient. He and Marie would meet and talk, and she'd stop by sometimes on her way home to visit with him. Purvis had met a girl at the wedding. Jill was one of the bridesmaids and was a nursing student at East Georgia. Purvis and she were getting pretty close, and he was spending most of his free time at Hank's and seeing her. While visiting Hank, he'd help him with repairs to the property.

Janet and Marie were staying in close contact. They talked almost every day about most anything, especially news about Hank. Janet told her, "He's beginning to read a lot on horse therapy programs and how they are helping vets cope with battle fatigue or post war depression problems. He sounds pretty excited about doing this."

"He told us the idea wasn't all that new. Prisoners throughout the US had been providing care to animals for years. Taking care of animals had changed even the most hardened of hearts. The juvenile justice system had farms, where residents took care of animals. Kids who had never learned how to love, or were loved, were finding love raising and caring for animals. Horses had helped socialize vets with severe psychological problems in several programs. This is what he seems to really want to do."

Hank, meanwhile, had been calling local banks trying to and arrange for a loan. Most of these banks didn't have a clue about what he was talking about. He would take the loan officers literature explaining what he wanted to do and nobody seemed interested in helping him. All they saw was a disabled veteran, and wanted to know what kind of collateral he had. They also wanted to know what kind of business experience he had or if he had any formal training in the area.

Hank was getting discouraged again. He told Marie, "No bank seems to want to help me. Even the VA is dragging it out. What will I do? How will I be able to take care of you if you come home?"

He drove home to share his frustrations with his family. He asked his dad, "How can I expect Marie to come home when I can't even provide for her?"

Jim answered, "I've already told you how. It's time you grow up and stop running away every time something doesn't go your way! You're married, and it's time to buckle down and take responsibility. You don't have any more excuses. I told you, you don't even have to work with all your benefits and Marie working. Why do you insist on worrying and hurting the people you love? There's no problem too big for God, so hand your troubles over to Him. It's not all about you anymore!"

Hank was a little taken back by his dad's response for him to grow up and be a man. Purvis, who had overheard the conversation, suggested they take a road trip. "Let's go to the coast or the mountains and try to sort things out. Sounds to me you need to take a break and screw your head back on," he said.

Hank said, "No man, I just want to go home now and try to figure out what's going on with my life. Dad laid it on pretty heavy this time."

Purvis called Buck, in Dothan, and told him, "Hank's in a really bad way. He's been separated from Marie, dropped out of college, and is feeling sorry for himself. He's having a hard time getting a loan for his horse therapy program, and is really pretty pitiful now."

Buck said, "Think I have something that will cheer him up. I've about finished the panel and will bring it over in a couple of weeks. Don't tell him. We'll just surprise him."

Well, Buck kept his promise and drove over from Dothan in the panel truck. He picked Purvis up and headed to Adrian. Hank had no clue they were coming until he saw a panel truck driving up to the house. Buck had turned that old '53 into a rolling tribute to the crew of Alvin's Huey.

Hank took one look at it and couldn't believe his eyes. Buck had customized it into one bad looking panel. "I've put a 350 cubic-inch big block V-8 in it with fuel injection, a posi-traction rear end, disc brakes, a Camaro front suspension and duel exhaust on her."

Hank was almost speechless. He started to tear up and could only say, "Damn, I think I'm going to cry."

Buck wasn't finished. "See how I painted her light Army green with black bumpers and black wide-angle wheels and rims. Look at the right panel. I had a guy paint a Huey providing fire cover for an LZ, and on the left panel he painted a Huey being loaded with a liter and wounded. On the back doors, I've put the names of the crew with 'Hooah' at the top of one door and 'Never Forget,' at the top the other door. Just look at the American flag on the hood," he boasted.

Hank was beginning to cry and could only manage to say, "Damn. Damn, she's beautiful."

Hank, Buck and Purvis took it for a spin over to the Dublin VA, to show it off. All the patients and staff thought it looked great. Just for a moment, they felt proud to have served. Then they took it to Marie's family, and to the VFW in Swainsboro. "It's beautiful", everyone said. Marie's dad said, "This is one heck of a tribute Buck. You should be proud of your work. I know Alvin and the crew are smiling down on you and feeling real proud, too."

Buck couldn't restrain himself anymore and told them how he wanted to have a replica of a M-60 that could face out the rear doors ready to fire. He also wanted to put brochures and other information about Vietnam organizations on the inside. "Maybe I can have a monitor showing Huey's in action in Nam, so that people can see what all they did. It would really be a rolling tribute then."

Hank said, "I can put different animal therapy resource material and veteran contact numbers inside, telling them where to get help."

Buck said, "I want us to take it to some of the other VA's and military bases in the area. Take it to VFWs, American Legion Posts and put it in parades. I want people to never forget about the Vietnam war and what it meant." Everyone agreed to help any way they could to keep the tribute alive.

Janet called Marie and told her, "Buck's trip was a real success. Hank called us right afterwards and was so excited about the truck and the visit. You know, he really wants to achieve his goals and have you come back, I think. He told me how much he missed you."

A couple of nights after the visit, Hank decided to get a six pack and celebrate. He passed a Camp Meeting sign outside off town which read, "Come Learn About The 3-C's and 3-S's in The Bible".

He later told Sam, one of patients from the VA, who was helping him with some chores around the barn, "I don't know why I decided to go. Maybe it was divine intervention or my father 's words, but I went. The evangelist started out the first night recalling his childhood, 'I can remember telling all my friends that my dad gave me this or that. What dad doesn't want to give his children whatever they want? He reminded us that as our heavenly Father, God wants only the best for us. The Bible tells us, "I shall not want,"' he continued.

"Sam, I remembered Robert telling us, in Nam, about how his dad went out and bought him a 1954 Oldsmobile, just because he told him he wanted it. 'Dad went right up to that house and asked the owner if he would sell it and he bought it for me,' Robert said. Heck, I even remember when my dad bought me my first gun, just because I asked for it," Hank added.

"The preacher told us about how he overcame self-pity and worthlessness after he turned his stress over to the Lord. 'I wasn't eating, sleeping or able to hold down a job until I asked God to let His care handle my stress. I had heard a radio program where a preacher quoted some scripture which read, 'Surely goodness and mercy will follow you all the days of your life,'" he concluded.

"Hey, isn't that what your old man told you when you were home last time? Sounds like he was right on," Sam replied.

"On the last evening, the evangelist talked about how difficult it was trying to handle his newly found success. 'When things are going well we tend to forget how we got there. Success can lead to sin and to a prideful heart if you let it. Remember, God wants us living on the top of the water and not be bottom feeders. When we look good He looks good, especially when we tell others He made it all possible. So, give God the glory and let His control will handle your success and His cross handle your sins,'" he told us.

Sam said, "It sounded like a pretty good camp meeting."

"Sam, it was a great three nights full of good words and singing old time gospel music. I finally realized why Alvin was thanking Jesus. He was thanking Him for taking him out of hell and receiving him into His heavenly arms. I decided right then and there to turn everything I had over to the Lord and let Him handle it! I'm going to make Marie, my family, and friends proud of me."

Hank would often ride over to the Dublin VA just to visit with fellow vets. It was also a good time to talk up his horse therapy program to anyone who would listen.

One day he met Anthony who, he later learned, had survived a mortar attack near Quang Tri up on the DMZ (Demilitarized Zone), and had flown several chopper missions. "My job was to escort aircraft carrying troops to landing zones, and make sure the LZ's were safe. Machine guns and rockets were used to clear the area before we dropped the guys off. I even escorted medevac missions," he said.

He told Hank that, back on base, "We dug our own bunkers next to our beds so we could roll over into them when rounds came in. It only took about a week to figure out the difference between incoming and outgoing rounds."

"Even though I was a pilot, I often found myself helping with the fueling of the Huey. One day I took off my fireproof gloves. The fuel splashed up into the chopper's turbine, causing a big backfire. I often didn't shut down the helicopter during a combat situation or when near a fuel cell, just in case I had to bug out.

"The fireproof suit didn't burn, but the vapors did, and my hands and body were pretty badly burned. An Airforce helicopter that was nearby landed and the medic came over and put a blanket on me to put out the flames. The chopper flew me out to the hospital ship REPOSE, because the fumes got into my suit and caught fire. I was in pretty bad shape. After a couple of days on the ship, I was sent to Japan, where I spent ten days before returning to the states."

Hank said, "That had to be terrible, catching fire like that. I'm glad you are ok now and living a productive life. Thanks for your service."

Easter was spent with Marie's family. They enjoyed seeing all the children in their Easter outfits running around the church. It was a lovely day and was their first Easter together since being separated. Hank was really beginning to miss her. He was ready for them to get back together. She had stayed by his side despite all his short comings and problems. Marie had invited him to church that Easter and he decided to ask her to come home. So, after lunch he helped her pack a few items and they headed to the little dogtrot in Adrian.

THANK YOU JESUS

Hank got a small loan from his father-in-law, who also found him a couple of calm rescue horses. At that time, there was not one set standard for a therapy horse, or one best breed. They came from many different sources and a wide variety of backgrounds. Some came with debilitating physical ailments like lameness or allergies, while others came from the Florida race tracks and were incapable of racing anymore.

Pepper Jack was the first horse Jim found for Hank. He came from a rescue facility in Florida that rehabilitated older, retired racers. Pepper Jack was an extremely good- natured horse that appeared happy not to be racing anymore. He was gentle and not easily spooked. He worked well with a leader and a side walker, and was responsive to commands and tolerant of mistakes. He didn't try to bite or kick his handlers or eat the fence post.

Spots, the second horse, came from a farm near Swainsboro. She had been raised from a colt by the farmer's daughter. She was an easy rider and tended to get along with every situation. Spots was sort of laid back and seemed to have a sixth sense when it came to being around troubled vets. Under Spots patient tutelage, she helped in the recovery of several veterans.

Thankfully, the horses came with tack. Marie took it upon herself to see that the tack fit properly, that the saddles weren't rubbing, or the girth too tight and the bits weren't inverted. She went at this like the trained occupational therapist she was. She set up regular veterinary, farrier, and dental schedules. She realized that a happy horse was a great horse for therapy.

Marie and Hank attended Memorial Day in Willacoochee with his family. The day was filled with a parade, a BBQ, a watermelon eating contest, and awards for those who could spit the watermelon seeds the furthest. He and Marie had just recently ended their short separation and he was happy to have her back by his side.

Purvis helped Hank expand a small barn and build a corral. The original barn wasn't much more than a 20'x14' wooden structure. Purvis helped build another 10' onto it which included a tack room. He also helped divide it into four stalls, and he enlarged the corral to handle up to six horses. They both hoped that one day they would need to expand again.

With his new commitment, to let God care handle all his stress, things were turning around. He and Marie were happily back together. He realized just how much he had missed her. She had remained by his side during Armed Forces Day, Memorial Day and Veterans Day activities. Marie, along with some of the mental health physicians at the VA, were sending him patients now. Hank seemed more at peace with his feelings after attending all those celebrations. The local VFWs provided man power to help him add another small room to the barn. The room could hold four single metal framed beds and included a small bathroom and a kitchen. This would allow up to four vets to stay at one, time while passing through the area or participating in the therapy program. Most of the men were sent from the VA or VFWs in the area. No one could smoke, drink alcohol, or carry a weapon while staying there. Occupants could stay up to four weeks, and were responsible for keeping the area clean and fending for themselves. They also handled chores like feeding the horses, fixing fences, or whatever else was needed in return for their free room and board. They were also expected to help with the patients participating in the program.

The in-house residents also had to sign a waiver for any injuries they might receive while staying there. They were expected to attend a Wednesday night prayer program which was held in the barn and was overseen by a local men's bible class. A Gideon supplied Hank with some Bibles for those staying there. Several of the vets found employment while there.

The surrounding cities of Adrien, Swainsboro, and Dublin were slowly recognizing what was going on out at Hank's place. Some Sunday school classes adopted the program and provided bath items like towels, soap, tooth brushes, and tooth paste. Area stores pitched in with deodorants and shaving items. The VFWs, American Legion Posts, and other civic organizations provided needed labor, rounded up building supplies, and helped out monetarily. It was all in an effort to say thank you for all that these veterans had done, and to give them the proper welcome home they deserved.

Hank met a vet one day at the VA while he was waiting in the lobby for Marie to join him for lunch. His name was Patrick and he was traveling the country to find a place to settle. When Marie came down, Hank introduced Pat to her and invited him to lunch with them.

At lunch, Pat told them he was headed south to find a place to call home. He had been in Nam about the same time as Hank, and they hit it off almost immediately. Marie and Hank shared how they met and later married. When lunch was over, they invited Pat to stay with them for a while and see how the horse therapy program worked. Pat gladly accepted and went out to stay with them.

Pat was average height, thin but solid. He didn't look much like a hero. But what did heroes look like? Hank thought. He was from California and knew all about the hippie generation and what the war objectors were all about; 'Love not war'. He said, "It was hard coming home and not being able to wear my uniform. It was hard hearing people call us, 'baby killers'. I'm traveling the country trying to find a place to light, and stopped in here to get a few prescriptions filled." Over the coming days. Hank learned that Pat had received three Purple Hearts, a Silver Star and the Army Commendation Medal for Heroism with "V" Device during his time in Vietnam. He had been an Army medic and was a true hero. Eventually, Pat told Hank how he earned the awards.

He said, "A couple of Purple Hearts came from the same event. Our unit ran into a NVA HQ with a 3-story underground hospital. Lost all but 8 members of the 2nd platoon-including the medic. I was in Charlie Company, 3rd platoon." Pat was being very modest. He later showed Hank a copy of his Silver Star Award which told the rest of the story. It read:

Reason: "For gallantry in action: Private First Class Walters distinguished himself by heroic actions on 22 November 1968, while serving with the Company C, 1st Battalion, 27th Infantry in the Republic of Vietnam. While on a combat Operation, Company C came in contact with a large enemy force. During the ensuing battle, the beleaguered unit sustained several casualties. Although the hostiles were directing their fire towards him, Private Walters, with complete disregard for his own safety, exposed himself to deadly Viet Cong shelling as he moved throughout the enemy kill zone administering life saving first aid to the injured. After carrying his fallen comrades to a relatively secure area, Private Walters prepared the wounded for the evacuation helicopter. His actions were responsible for saving several lives and the success of the mission. Private Walters' personal bravery, aggressiveness, and devotion to duty are in keeping with the highest traditions of the military service and reflect great credit upon himself, his unit, the 25th Infantry Division and the United States Army."

Wow, Hank thought. No wonder he calls November his second birthday. "I'm still carrying some shrapnel from that one," he said.

"The Army commendation with 'V': for valor device was earned on the night of February 22-23, 1969 during-Tet '69, where I also got another Purple Heart." He told Hank. Again, he was being modest. He showed Hank a copy of his Award Of The Army Commendation Medal For Heroism with 'V':

Reason: "For heroism in connection with military operations against a hostile Force: Specialist Four Walters distinguished himself by heroic actions on 23 February 1969, while serving with the Headquarters and Headquarters Company, 1st Battalion, 27th Infantry in the Republic of Vietnam. While on a sweep operation, Headquarters Company came under intense enemy attack. During the initial contact, several casualties were sustained. With complete disregard for his own safety, Specialist Walters moved through the bullet swept area to treat and evacuate the wounded soldiers to safety. Throughout the entire battle, Specialist Walters continued to administer first aid to the many wounded. His valorous actions were responsible for saving many lives. Specialist Walters personal bravery, aggressiveness and devotion to duty are in keeping with the highest traditions of the military service and reflect great credit upon himself, his unit, the 25th Infantry Division, and the United States Army."

"This was the Battle of Dau Tieng. Another frightening night," Pat said.

Hank could only think, wow, we have a true hero staying right here with us. He invited Marie's family and his family over to meet Pat. They had a big barbeque in his honor and everyone staying at the farm, along with some vets from the VA, attended.

During the visit, Pat told Purvis that, "At the Battle of Dau Tieng which started a little after midnight everybody from cooks, clerks, infantrymen, mechanics, engineers, and military police ended up fighting. The NVA had hit the base camp from four sides. They stormed the perimeter at two points and even got in through a tunnel. Hundreds of rounds of rockets, mortars and RPG's struck the camp. It was one hell of a fight. Helicopter gunships were making low level passes, pouring lead on the enemy. Air strikes shot their bombs right up to the perimeter, forcing the enemy to retreat. We lost a lot of good men on both sides during this one."

Later he told Purvis that he got his first Purple Heart in November 1968 and his second Purple Heart with oak leaf cluster in 1969. He went on to share some other thoughts of his time in Nam.

He said, "Down time was usually spent in either one or the other camp; drunk or stoned. I was usually in the drunk bunch. Nights on 'ambush' were very long, scary, and usually wet. Over the time there, I hauled out enough men to call 50 Dust Off missions. During those 10 month's I was on line either with the regular Infantry or with the 25th Division 1st Wolf Hounds Combined Recon Intell Platoon."

Pat stayed on for a couple of months helping Hank anywhere he could with the program. They saw vets coming together as brothers and overcoming their fears together.

Hank encouraged the vets in the program to swap stories about their time in Vietnam. He would usually start by telling them about his chopper crash and how he couldn't remember a lot about it. He could only recall that while they were providing air cover for a couple medevac choppers, their bird was hit by small arms. "Robert, our pilot, was killed instantly and then Dain, the co-pilot, got it next. Alvin, the other gunner was, then hit and as he fell into my arms, I heard him saying, "Thank You Jesus" as he died.

"The chopper kept falling out of control when RPG's hit it. I was wounded and didn't know whether to jump or not. All of a sudden, I either jumped or was blown out of the ship just seconds before it blew up. It was like some kind of divine intervention that saved my life."

Sharing war stories was part of the therapy program. The more they relived their story, the easier it got managing it. They realized they weren't alone in their turmoil, l and talking about it only helped to overcome their fear.

The physicians at the VA were impressed to see so much improvement in the patients they sent to Hank's program. Having someone to talk to them and listen to them was having amazing effects on those veterans. Several of the occupational and physical therapists asked their department heads to let them go to the center two times a week to work with the patients. One would take Monday and Wednesday, while the other would take Tuesday and Thursday. That way, someone was there to help oversee the therapy and hold group sessions. These OT's and PTs also volunteered as staff for the program and spent a great deal of their off time at the farm. They often took visitors around on tours of the property. The program could only handle four patients at the time, but Hank was able to secure two more horses and was looking for more. Mornings were dedicated to the horses, because it was usually cooler at that time in the summer. The guys usually spent this time grooming, walking, feeding, and bonding with the horses. In the afternoon, they attended group sessions or handled chores. The schedule reversed in the winter, when it tended to be warmer in the afternoon.

Hank remembered several military chaplains remark that if someone went into war without faith, they usually returned from war with it. It's amazing what goes on in a fox hole or bunker during the heat of war. He decided to paint a prayer on a piece of plywood and hang it on a wall in the bunk house:

"Lord, Grant me the serenity to accept the things I cannot change; the courage to change things I can and the wisdom to know the difference. Reinhold Niebuhr."

Hank figured he'd never know if this prayer helped anyone or not. He just hoped they would pray it daily as they continued on with their journey.

A county deputy was called to pick up a transient person at a club outside of Adrian. The club owner had called for a deputy because one of the patrons had had too much to drink. When the deputy arrived at the club, he found a VA card in the guy's wallet. The deputy was a vet and didn't want this guy getting into trouble. He called a VFW member and told him what was going on. The VFW member then called Hank to see if he had room in the bunk house for one more. Hank said to send him on out when he sobered up.

The deputy took Josh out to the farm and told Hank what he had learned so far. Josh had just arrived in Brunswick, Georgia, aboard a cargo ship from Japan. After unloading the supplies, the ship was going in for maintenance for a couple of months, and the crew was given this time off. Josh had been a cook aboard the freighter.

Josh seemed to be a pretty good guy when he sobered up. He was twenty and kind of squirrely and had been born in Columbia, South Carolina. His dad had been a cook in the Army and had served twenty years. Josh had been drafted and didn't want to fight, so he became a cook. He was grateful for a place to stay at the farm for a while. The other three members in the bunk house were glad to see him, especially when they learned he could cook. He soon won their affection by serving up good meals, even some incorporating SPAM into the dishes.

Josh overheard a group therapy session one day as the patients were talking about their war experiences. This somehow tripped Josh's memory and something happened to him. Later that night, he experienced a really bad nightmare. It was so bad that Hank had to call one of the psychiatrist at the VA for help. He agreed to go out to the farm and sedate Josh. He was a brother, and they didn't want him to get in trouble with the law. The next day he was seen at the VA in Dublin where he told his story.

"I was an Army cook at a fire base west of Da Nang. The base was overrun early one morning by sappers. They were hitting the base with satchel charges, mortars, RPG's, and anything else they had. Everyone, including myself, had to fight trying to defend the base. As the base was overrun, I was hit on the forehead and knocked out. When I woke up later that morning, I learned that only two of us had made it. The VC were gone and had destroyed the base on the way out. I must have had a breakdown. I was sent to the states, where they gave me a medical discharge. The Veterans Hospital in Augusta, Georgia, just gave me some pills and told me to follow up in a couple of months.

"I do pretty good when I'm not stressed out and when I stay on my medication. I was able to get a job on a freighter out of Savannah to Japan. It carried grain and other products from Georgia to Japan. I was a cook aboard her and did pretty good while at sea. I was able to stay pretty much to myself, and enjoyed the movement of the sea. There was no mention of war or war stories to set me off, so I had very few flash backs. Being on the sea gave me plenty of time to forget. I thought I was doing good until I heard some of the patients in a therapy session talking about their war experiences, and for some reason I had a flash back and I ended up here."

Josh stayed on at the farm for a little while and was getting back to his old self. His cooking was so good, the bunkhouse guys didn't want him to go. They were real sad to hear he was headed back to the Brunswick to sail the seas some more. Hank and Marie had enjoyed several of his meals and wanted him to stay. They even offered him a small salary with free room and board if he would stay. He would have been their first employee. Josh felt it was better to go and travel the world while he was still young and single before completing his journey home.

It was a special 4th of July for Hank because he was at home. He had spent his first one in the Fitzsimons Army Hospital in Colorado. Marie and he were so happy together and had driven down a couple days earlier to enjoy the holiday with his family. They cooked a feral hog as usual but, this time it was a little more subdued. Willard was not there to help with the cooking, and his stories were greatly missed. Hank remembered that Sunday in Nam, when he told his crew how they celebrated the Fourth back home; how the menfolk picked out a hog, gutted it, boiled the hair off of it and slow cooked it all night long until the meat would start to fall off. During the rest of the night they would sit around and tell stories of all kinds from hunting to fishing.

Buck and his wife had driven the panel over from Dothan. The next day they had a grand meal before heading to the parade where they showed off the truck to several hundred attendees. Everyone seemed to gather around the truck, and many remarked how great it looked. Some said it looked like a piece of art. The car buffs couldn't get over how low it sat, and that it had a beefed 350-cubic-inch fuel injected V-8 which just kind of hummed sitting there idling.

Buck drove it during the parade with Marie sitting proudly between him and Hank. Hank was busy waving at people along the route and watching out for the Shriners weaving go carts in and out. He started feeling better about himself and having served in Nam, as he saw people proudly waving the American flag. He saw old school mates, teachers, old school principals, and coaches cheering. He saw Bert and Mable standing there with Buck's wife and the rest of the family all waving flags. He couldn't help but think how glad he was that Bert hadn't died while he was in Nam, because they were still enjoying each other's company.

The panel was such a success that before Buck left for home he was asked, by the mayor, to bring it back the next year. Some of the towns he drove home through to Dothan also asked him to be in their parades. The crew would have been proud of them that day.

At the end of the parade, they all met up and said their goodbyes. Hank and Marie had decided to go home and watch the Boston Pops concert and make their own fire-works!

Christmas was spent at both parents' homes. Marie and he went to Willacoochee Christmas eve and celebrated Christmas morning exchanging gifts. After at a big brunch, they headed to visit with

Marie's family. They exchanged gifts and shared a traditional Christmas dinner. They sat down to a table filled with ham, turkey, stuffed dressing, mac and cheese, cranberry sauce, ambrosia, rice and gravy, collard greens, butter beans. To wash it all down, there was egg nog and sweet tea, the table wine of the south. Two big meals in one day was a bit much, so they decided they might alternate holidays the next year. They still had to go home and have some dessert with the guys in the bunk house.

Hank didn't want the program to get so big that it lost its intimacy. One-on-one between horse and veteran was still the best approach in this type therapy. The closer the bond, the better the result, was what he wanted. He knew that eventually he would have to hire some staff, which would require more funding. He went around the area giving talks to whoever would listen. He tried to stay within the Augusta, Macon, Savannah, Brunswick, and Valdosta circle. Both he and Marie were reading as much as they could to stay on top of this relatively new field.

The horses had a gentle way of calming a hardened heart. They were good listeners and didn't judge their handlers. The vets could talk to them about their hang-ups because there was no concern for rejection. The horses would nuzzle them and accept them for who they were. The vets wound up treating themselves while washing, grooming, walking, or riding the horses. The psychiatrists and psychologists who came out to visit were so impressed that they began to send more patients his way. Marie found herself getting interested in using the motion of the horses to conduct targeted therapy. The physical therapists at the VA were seeing increased muscle strength and coordination in the patients attending the riding program. Hank's program was treating not only the mental problems, but the physical problems many of the vets had. He made certain that the horses got plenty of turnout time in a pasture and trail riding time to ease their stress. He joined the North American Riding for

Handicapped Association out in Denver to stay current in this new
and exciting field of therapy.

Hank met another veteran named Park. "You can call me Bob,"
he said. He had heard about the horse therapy program and had driv-
en down from Augusta to check it out. He later told Hank that he had
been wounded during Operation Attleboro, November 4-5,1966,
and how the operation quickly changed from a minor search and
destroy mission into a major battle lasting from November 3rd to the
24th. It had become the first large-scale multi-unit operation of our
involvement in Vietnam. He and Hank became friends quickly and,
before he left, he shared some of his thoughts with him.

"It's a mental battle that many of us are trying to live through.
Many of us would like to forget the trauma and memories that haunt
us, but we can't. At the same time, the memories of friends and
brothers we lost is also there, and we should never forget them and
what they gave up. It is also important to realize that this isn't limit-
ed to Vietnam vets. So, we cry our hidden tears in quiet places when
we are alone, and pray that the pain will be eased."

He told Hank, "This is a good program and I will tell everyone I
know about it. Keep up the good work. It was great to meet you and
Marie. I hope we will stay in touch."

A guy phoned a few days later and asked if he could come down
and visit the program. Hank invited him on down. Jack was a Physician Assistant (PA), from North Carolina. He had attended the PA
Program at Duke University and graduated in 1969. The program
had been started by Dr. Eugene Stead Jr. in 1965. It started training
returning medics from Korea and Vietnam to assume some of the
duties performed by physicians. These wars had created a physician
shortage similar to that seen after WWII and Dr. Stead saw this as a
way to fill the void.

Jack had heard about Hank's Program and wanted to see it firsthand. He had served in Vietnam as a hospital corpsman on the hospital ship USS REPOSE, (AH-16). They shared stories and memo-

ries of their time there. They found out they had a lot in common. Jack, like Hank, was still having flashbacks and appreciated what the program had to offer. He saw firsthand how the vets were coming together while caring for the horses and each other. He also saw how Hank was able to overcome his own fears and was successful in this endeavor. "I'm going back and tell everyone about this program and, with your permission, I'd like to write a paper about it."

Hank answered, "That would be great, I need all the publicity I can get to let the veterans know I'm here. Why don't you take a few of these brochures along to give out?"

Not all the people he met at the VA were veterans with physical or medical problems. He met a guy named Daniel while getting lunch one day. He heard Daniel tell the person in front of him that he had been a civilian contractor in Da Nang. This interested Hank so much that he asked him sit with him during lunch. He learned that Daniel was from Eastman, Georgia, originally and was in Nam about the same time he was. Daniel was married and had two children. "I come here often to visit the patients, because I feel all you guys are getting a bum rap. I was over there and have a better understanding of what went on," he said. Hank decided to ask him out to the farm to learn about his therapy program.

That afternoon, he learned Daniel was one of several civilian contractors who worked in support roles in Nam. He had been sent Camp Tien Sha, the Navy supply depot in Da Nang. While waiting to go over, the company gave him some material on the depot to help him understand what he was getting into. He learned that the port, in Da Nang, controlled around 900,000 square feet of supply depot space. There was 2.7 million square feet of open refrigerated space. He read where the port handled 320,000 tons of cargo each year, and had 2 fuel tank farms reaching a capacity of 50 million gallons. "I thought to myself that's a big depot. I don't want to bore you," he said. "It's just that I don't get many chances to share my experiences with someone." Hank told him to carry on, so Daniel proceeded. "The company brochure read that there were 450 officers, 10,000 sailors, and a civilian work force of 11,000 Vietnamese and civilian contractors.

"The depot supplied over 200,000 US, Vietnamese and allied forces fighting in the 1 Corps Zone in northern Vietnam with everything they needed to combat the VC and NVA. When I got there, I had never before seen such a collection of supplies, in one place. There was food, fuel, ammunition, weapons, toilet paper, and even tooth paste stored everywhere. The area smelled of diesel fuel and things rotting from the heat, and along with the constant sound of choppers in the air, it was a hard place to forget," he added.

They took a break for dinner, where Daniel met Marie. She, too, seemed intrigued to meet a civilian who had spent time in Vietnam. After dinner, they went down to the barn, and Daniel continued his memories. He recalled that it was a logistical nightmare at times. "Imagine two shifts, of around 6,000 people per shift, running around stocking, distributing and restocking supplies 24/7.

"Early one morning, around 1 am, the depot got hit by what sounded like hundreds of mortars and rockets. All hell was breaking loose. The electricity was knocked out, fires started burning uncontrollably, while people ran in every direction trying to get out. The warehouses were being destroyed one-by-one. I happened to be in one as the roof collapsed. You couldn't see in the dark, but you could hear the screams of trapped burning people. The area was hit all morning. There was a storage tank filled with agent orange that blew. It was a devastating blow to the depot. Tons of cargo were blown up. Hundreds of people injured or killed. I wasn't injured physically, but still don't like to hear fireworks going off," he ended.

After hearing Daniel's experience, the guys accepted him as one of their own. Maybe he hadn't served in the military, in Nam, like they did, but he was a veteran just the same. Daniel asked Hank, "Have you ever thought how this program could help people like me?"

Hank replied, "That certainly is something to think about, isn't it? I'll see what's out there." Daniel thanked Hank for the great visit and headed for Eastman. It was the beginning of a close friendship. He would bring his family over to go horseback riding on weekends and talk to the veterans.

People from all over the southeast were now sending money to help defray the cost of his Horse Therapy Program. Hank was able to expand the center, and overcome his own fears. The banks were now willing to lend money if he needed it.

Marie came home one day and told Hank, "You're going to be a daddy." Hank couldn't believe his ears and said, "A what?" Marie said, "A daddy. I'm about eight weeks pregnant. Isn't it going to be great! God is really providing for us now. I'm so happy."

After hearing the good news, Hank decided he needed to add a nursery. He and Purvis put up some walls in the parlor side of the house to make a small nursery. In less than eight months, he was going to be a daddy.

Pat had written to tell them he had decided to become a Physician Assistant. He had made his way to Kentucky, and had been accepted into the University's PA Program. He was excited to be in a career where he could take care of veterans and their many challenges.

Purvis and Jill had decided to set a wedding date. She was getting close to graduating as a nurse, and her income would come in handy. Not only was she beautiful and loved Purvis, she would have a job upon graduation. She had applied for a job in Willacoochee and at several other clinics in Waycross. Certainly, someone would want to hire her. The thought of having a place to move into with fifteen acres, was a great start for them.

Janet had met a young guy from Valdosta, who was attending college there. They were getting pretty close, and she entertained leaving Willacoochee after all. Whit was his name and he wanted to become a hospital administrator one day. Where they would live was still pretty much up in the in the air. With Moody Airforce base so nearby, he thought about joining the Air Force and letting them pay for any extra degrees he might need. That meant they could be living most anywhere and Janet was excited about that prospect.

Hank called the family and told them how Marie had been shopping for draperies and other baby items. "She is going to paint the nursery pink and is so excited. I told her to let me paint it because she doesn't need to be straining herself like that. She can be stubborn at times and even finds time to help me with the horses. She's been reading about how to keep them happy! Won't be long now."

After the birth of his daughter, Louise, Hank began to reflect over the past couple of years. He saw where he really wasn't alone during his recovery. His family had never given up on him. He remembered all the times his mother had told him "to let God handle things."

He remembered his father telling him in no uncertain terms, "It's time you grow up and stop running away every time something doesn't go your way! You're married and it's time to buckle down and take responsibility. You don't have any more excuses."

He recalled attending the Camp Meeting outside Adrian for three days where, the evangelist had told those in attendance how God wants only the best for them. "He's our Heavenly Father, and what father doesn't want the best for his children." He told them how to overcome self-pity and worthlessness by letting God's care handle our stress and letting His control handle our successes. "When we look good, He looks good." His life began to change for the better after attending this Camp Meeting where he decided to let God live in him and to live for others. He took 'self' out of the equation.

He realized that his program wasn't just for veterans suffering from physical and mental challenges. It could help anyone, like Daniel, who wanted help. Alcoholics, drug addicts, battered persons, abused children, and depressed people could all find some help from this type therapy. He kept resource material on hand for several agencies just in case someone showed up needing help.

Hank thanked God for providing for his family's daily needs, and that Marie had remained by his side. He thanked Him for his beautiful daughter, and for letting him help veterans. This part of his journey home was complete the day he handed his daughter over to the open arms of her grandfather and heard himself saying, "Thank You Jesus."

ACKNOWLEDGEMENT

The "A Long Journey Home" would not have been possible without the help of several people who contributed to this work of semi-fiction. They provided memories and stories from personal experiences while serving in The Republic of Vietnam, in various capacities. I have listed them in the order in which they appear in the book:

Daniel "Danny" R. Pilgrim, E4, Huey Crew Chief, $1^{st}/7^{th}$ Air CAV Company, Pit Vipers, Bin Long, Mekong Delta, Republic of Vietnam 1968-69.

Ron Henson, Sargent, Don Binh Than, Republic of Vietnam, 1969-70.

Patrick T. Walters, Sp4, Medic, Charlie Company, 1st Battalion, 3rd Platoon. 27th Infantry, 25th Infantry Division, Republic of Vietnam, 1968-69. Awarded: The Silver Star, Three Purple Hearts, and The Army Commendation Medal for Heroism with "V" Device. LTC USAR, Retired.

Robert Park, Buck Sgt. E-5, 11B20 (Infantry) 25th Infantry Division at Cu Chi, Republic of Vietnam, A Company, 2nd Battalion, 27th Infantry Regiment, Jan. 1966- Nov. 1966. "I arrived as a PFC, and when I was sent back the end of Nov.1966, I was a Buck Sgt. E-5. I had been wounded during Operation Attleboro (Nov. 4-5). We were called the Wolfhounds."

Robert "Bobby" W. Hawes, SK2, Covered Storage, Camp Tien Sha, Da Nang, Republic Of Vietnam, 1968-69. Retired USNR with 22 years of service.

These are some of the true heroes of the war, and each generously contributed to this work.

"Hooah" and "Hooyah"!

While the Vietnam War is a fact, Hank's story grew out of my imagination and my service as a hospital corpsman, in Vietnam, stationed aboard the USS REPOSE(AH-16), Hospital Ship, 1969-70. All the other characters in the book are fictional, except for the veterans listed above.

I especially want to acknowledge my wife, Debbie, who helped edit, and put up with me during the many hours of writing and re-writing this work. She has also put up with me for 46 years, and makes me look good. Kudos, also go out, to my daughter Jennifer and her husband Scott for their help in the finished work.

ABOUT THE AUTHOR

Born in Pennsylvania and educated in Georgia, Winston H. Hunt received his Bachelor of Science degree from the School of Allied Health Sciences at the Medical College of Georgia in Augusta.

He has been married to Deborah for forty-six years and has two daughters, two grandsons and three granddogs.

He served as a Hospital Corpsman in Vietnam aboard the Hospital Ship USS REPOSE (AH-16). He is the author of "A Half Bubble Out of Plumb."

He is retired, after working nearly fifty years in the health care field, as a Physician Assistant, Pharmaceutical Rep and Trainer, and an Assistant Professor. He spends his time camping, writing books, and picking up pine cones so they don't clog up his mower.

AFTERWORD

Daniel "Danny" R. Pilgrim returned from Vietnam and joined his father in the auto repair business. He now owns the shop and his 3 sons are working with him. Rose and he also have 3 girls and 10 grandchildren. He enjoys classic old cars and motorcycling in the mountains.

Ron Henson spent 35 years in manufacturing mainly in management positions. He has 3 children and 4 grandchildren, and shared a few last thoughts with me. Ron had met Mickey Frownfelter from Lawrence, Kansas, while in basic training at Fort Campbell, Kentucky. They remained friends throughout the entire Vietnam experience.

"We DROS's back to the U.S. in January, 1970, with orders to report to Fort Hood, Texas for sweeping and mopping floors for the rest of our enlistment. We landed in Seattle at 1:00am. Mickey and I were half asleep when a big burley Drill Sergeant came by, tapped my shoes and asked me if we wanted to be Drill Sergeants. The burley E-8 said we would receive special uniforms, $50.00 extra pay per month and our choice of basic training center. I nudged Mickey and said, let's go to Fort Campbell. So, as they say, we loaded up our gear and spent 6 weeks at Fort Jackson, South Carolina, training for our new vocation and then headed for Fort Campbell,

"We "greeted" new recruits every eight weeks. We "welcomed" five buses to our barracks to begin their matriculation into the US Army. Over the next year and a half, at Fort Campbell, we had a diversity of ethnic personnel. Some were farm boys from Iowa, some were Reservists from Minnesota and some were from the south side Chicago ghettos."

"When Jeannie and I left the military, after a short stay in Wabash, Indiana, we moved to Canada."

While in Canada he said, "I received a call one morning from a student in the local high school journalism class. The student asked for an interview because of the three United Aircraft plants in Ontario I was the only US citizen working there that had served in Vietnam. They wanted my opinion of feelings toward my service. To my regret, I acquiesced. I wanted to get the point across that not all Americans came to Canada to avoid the draft and escape serving in Vietnam.

"When the three acned adolescents sat down with me, it was over. The first, and last, question I took was in two parts: 'What was my view of Mei Lei and how many babies did you kill in Vietnam?' I told them to practice hockey and get the puck out of here!"

"Reckon that's why I'm in anger management classes."

Patrick T. Walters is a retired Physician Assistant and living in the mountains of North Carolina. He is enjoying being a grandparent and traveling the world with his wife Nancy. They have 2 children and 2 grandchildren. He is also a retired LTC USAR.

Robert Park is a retired teacher who used to breed dogs, all black German Shepherds. He has 3 sons, 7 grandchildren and 2 great grandchildren.

Bobby Hawes is retired after 37 years with J&J and 8 years with Allstate Insurance Company. He is retired after 22 years of service in the USNR. He has 2 children and 2 granddaughters.

Not long ago, I got reacquainted with a childhood friend I found on Facebook. We had lunch together and shared some of our memories from Vietnam. I asked Bobby if he would like me to include some of his stories in this book. He replied, "I've told them hundreds of times, maybe I should write them down."

Weeks later, he came to my door with a large white envelope filled with memories. As he read his story aloud to Debbie, my wife, and me, he showed an aerial picture of the Tien Sha Base he was assigned to. I saw a 73- year old man returning to the 22- year old who was stationed there.

The pitch in his voice and the excitement of showing us where his barracks was on the picture was clear. "Look, that's Monkey Mountain, China Beach, the ammo dump over there, the Chief's quarters here, and that's the beach the Marines first landed on in Vietnam," he said. As he continued reading his memories his voice changed and started to crack at times, and tears welled up in his eyes. Bobby is just one of the approximately 850 thousand service men and women alive today who served in country. Everyone who served has his or her own memories and each has a journey home. This is Bobby's story:

"My story begins as a 22- year old Business Major, and senior, at Augusta College. I had only one course to complete, Statistics, before graduation. I had already joined the U.S. Navy Reserves and was scheduled to go on active duty in June of 1968. My plan was to take Statistics during Winter Quarter '68 and then go on active duty. I wanted to take Statistics last, because at AC, 70% of the students flunked it the first time, and I could work during Spring Quarter and repeat the course if I didn't pass it.

"I then took the Navy OCS test at Fort Jackson, South Carolina, and passed. They told me I'd be going to the Navy OCS in April. I asked them to let me wait until June, just in case I didn't pass Statistics the first time. They agreed to my request. I then took Statistics during Winter Quarter and passed it! I was so proud of becoming a college graduate and would soon be in the Navy OCS, Newport, Rhode Island.

"I notified the Navy about my accomplishment and they told me that the requirement for a passing score had been increased by 5 points and that I would have to retake the test! I retook the test and made the same identical score as the first time. So, no OCS and no commission. I had never been so disappointed in my life. I would be the first person, ever, in my family not to be a commissioned Naval Officer! Not being commissioned, which required 4 years of active duty, would end up being the greatest blessing in the world for me! I will explain later.

"June 15th, 1968: I am off to the US Naval Station in San Diego, California. I spent 14 days in transit, waiting for assignment orders. During that time, I met 2 young guys – George Grant, from Clinton, South Carolina, and Fred Pfohl, from Greensboro, North Carolina, who have been dear friends for life. George would even be in my wedding 2 years later. Our orders finally came through and the Master Chief said, 'They all read the same – Navy Support, Da Nang. Are there any questions? 'I responded that I had never heard of no ship "Navsupport Da Nang"! He replied, "Lad, it ain't no ship – you are going to be with the Marines at Da Nang, Vietnam!' "Oh Lord!"

"We spent three months in San Diego and Coronado, and a week at Camp Pendleton. Camp Pendleton is a Marine base, north of San Diego, where we went through survival school. It consisted of survival, evasion and resistance to interrogation training. The Marines were tough on us and they really meant business. The day we checked into Pendleton, it had to be over 100 degrees. They gave us each 2 blankets. My question was, what are these blankets for? 'Just wait, you'll see,' replied the Marines. I thought I was going to freeze to death that night. You would not believe how cold it gets in the desert. I was fortunate enough to get on the instructor's good side early on with the M-79 on the firing range. My first shot landed in the middle of a 55- gallon drum and blew it to pieces. I received immediate accolades and they left me alone. It was just dumb luck!

"When we got back to Coronado, we got wonderful news telling us that we would not have to go through the P.O.W./ Escape portion of the training and that we had 30 days leave. They said, 'We could go anywhere in the world we wanted to but you better be back at Norton AFB, San Bernardino, California, on September 12th 1968.' I looked over at George, he smiled and pointed east. The next day we got a $99.00 round trip airplane ticket from San Diego to Augusta, Georgia, for 30 days leave.

"The morning of Sept. 12, 1968, George and I met at Bush Field, Augusta, Georgia. George still teases me to this day about my mother bringing a roll of quarters to put in the flight insurance machine at the airport. You would have thought she was playing the slot machines.

"We spent the afternoon at Norton Air Force Base waiting for the 6pm flight to Da Nang. Many ladies' clubs were present serving sandwiches, pastries and desserts. When it came time to board the plane, we walked through these large swinging doors that had a large sign above them saying, "Through these doors pass America's Finest." Finally, at 8pm California time, 224 Navy and Marines took off for Da Nang, Vietnam. We had two stops in route, thank God. The first was at Hickam AFB, Honolulu, and the second stop was at Kadena AFB, Okinawa, site of some of the biggest battles in World War II. Kadena was as busy as Hartsfield Jackson in Atlanta, with all the flights coming and going to Vietnam.

"The last leg on into Da Nang is something that I will never forget as long as I live. I prayed, prayed asking God to please let me survive this ordeal and return home safely. The sun comes up and the plane is on a gradual decent into Da Nang. You could look out of the window and see aircraft carriers, cruisers, destroyers, and commercial ships. About that time the pilot comes on and says, 'Gentlemen, it has been an honor bringing you into Da Nang. Good luck to you, don't try to be a hero, God speed and we will see you this time next year.' With that the wheels hit the runway. I almost passed out. An armed forces policeman got on the stretch 8 and said, 'On behalf of General Creighton W. Abrams, we want to welcome you to Rocket City and the Republic of Vietnam.'

"They put us on cattle cars (18 wheeler trucks) and hauled us through the most god forsaken looking place that I had ever seen, with men and women were urinating on the street, to the old French base camp Tien Sha at the base of Monkey Mountain, where I would live for the next 12 months. They split us up at that point and some of the men I would not see again until the flight home one year later.

"I was assigned to covered storage as a store keeper striker. It was comparable to the largest Walmart in the world with 13,000 Navy and Marines assigned to it. George went to the Navy Hospital out on Monkey Mountain as a postal clerk and Fred was assigned to a Civic Action Team working out in the bush.

"I was dreading being away from home for the upcoming Holidays, but Aunt Iris's famous pound cake, along with reading hundreds of children's school cards, and the best Christmas dinner I ever ate made the time as special as it could be. The Navy topped it off on New Year's Eve '68 by firing flares all night. I'll bet the Navy spent one million dollars, at least, on the flares that cost $24.71 each. At the same time, the Battleship "New Jersey" shot it's guns all night long. Every time it would fire, my rack would come up off the floor.

"I would spend the rest of my tour as a storekeeper dispersing everything that was needed by the Marines from barrels of agent orange and ammunition, to clothing, food, lumber, and medicine. You name it, we had it! During the day, it was as safe as being in Augusta, but at night you know what would hit the fan!

"During my 12 months, we would receive approximately 45- 50 mortar and rocket attacks. There were 2 major attacks on us during my year. The first being on Feb. 23, 1969, during the TET offensive and the second on September 6, 1969, just 7 days before my scheduled departure.

"In late January, 1969, I was transferred to the night shift 7pm to 7am. I was very happy about this because the only time we had rocket attacks was at night and I would be able to get to the bunker in a shorter period of time. No more being woken up from a deep sleep. The night that I knew that I was definitely a Christian, and had definitely been saved, was the night of February 23, 1969. Around 2:30 am a barrage of rockets came in from everywhere. They successfully hit our camp ammo dump, which was less than a thousand yards from our work area. All work locations had assigned bunker locations which held 30 people. It was our ammunition that was going off, and it went on for 3 days. Imagine for a minute being inside a steel box with 29 other people. Most of the Vietnamese who worked with us cried all night long the first night. Each bunker had a boss and all were First Class Boatswain Mates (the mean guys) and they meant business. This one particular Vietnamese Papa San could not stop crying and screaming and our BMI – Ridley Bain from Spokane, Washington, who could speak fluent Vietnamese finally had to knock Papa San unconscious. Thank God, the crying and screaming was over.

"During the night of the second day, the sandbags 3 to 4 feet deep had been ripped open by the shelling and it was now metal on metal. Imagine being in a garbage can with someone beating on it with a baseball bat. Everybody got on the floor and prayed almost like the world was soon coming to an end for all of us. I curled up in a corner and began remembering my childhood, my family, friends, and especially my home church, First Baptist Church, Augusta, GA. All of a sudden, a warm radiating feeling came over me and I knew that I was going to be OK. God was definitely in my presence. I cannot wait to go to heaven and experience that feeling again!

"After the second night, the odor of urine and feces was almost too much to bear. Around 10am on the morning of February 25, the Marines came in and got us into armored personnel carriers and carried us to China Beach, where hot food and drink was waiting. I must have drunk 3 or 4 Cokes. While there, I ran into George and asked him to write my mother in Augusta and tell her I was all right. My mother kept that letter and I still have it today.

"January 3,1969: I received a phone call from the USO office at Camp Tien Sha asking me to come immediately to their office. They would not tell me what for over the phone. I had no idea what was going on. I took out for Tien Sha, in a rain storm, 3 miles away. I had a pass which got me through all security check points. Arriving at Tien Sha, soaking wet, I walked into the Chaplain's office and he asked me, 'Who is M. B. Giddens?' I told him he was my uncle who helped raise me. The Chaplain told me, 'I'm sorry to inform you that he has died.' He had been a very successful insurance agent and owned the largest insurance agency in Milledgeville, Georgia. At my college graduation ceremony, the previous June, he asked me to move to Milledgeville and join him in the insurance agency when I got out of the Navy. I came very close to going home on emergency leave, but because he was not blood kin, they would not allow it. There went my career in the insurance business!

"During the course of the balance of my tour, I enjoyed a 5 day, R&R in Tokyo, Japan with Fred. What a great trip we had. While there, former President Dwight David Eisenhower, who I deeply admired, died. I still have the "Time" magazine with all the funeral pictures that I purchased in Tokyo. We took a bus trip to Lake Kyoto, which is located at the base of Mount Fujiyama, and rode the highspeed train back to Tokyo. Fred bought the biggest camera that I had ever seen. We also bought stereo equipment and food. I even bought a pair of pearl earrings for my future wife, whoever she would be. This was in April and the cherry blossoms were in full bloom. I remember how cold it was. What a change from Da Nang! Getting on the plane to go back to Da Nang was tough.

"When we returned, newly elected President Richard Nixon withdrew 25,000 Marines from Da Nang. I will never forget the morning when the Marines came riding by our compound in their tanks and armored personnel caravans. Each tank was flying some type of flag and many were flying rebel flags. They were on their way to Deep Water Piers to get on ships to be transported to Subic Bay, in the Philippines. By the way, former Heisman Trophy winner Roger Staubach worked at Deep Water Piers.

"Before I left Da Nang, we had to go through the Ted Kennedy, Mary Jo Kopechne – Chappaquiddick Island fiasco. My mother wrote me a 17- page letter explaining all of that and I bet that I knew about it before she did. God bless her!

"I heard a live transmission from America on the landing on the Moon on July 20, 1969. Everybody was so excited! How in the world can a country who put a man on the Moon not win this war in S.E. Asia?

"The final hurrah was the death of Ho Chi Min. I had 8 days to go in country. The Vietnamese blew covered storage almost to hell and back. On 9-6-69 we were informed that the Vietnamese had a plan to overrun our compound. They brought in both shifts of men and put 2 men each in foxholes which surrounded our compound, preparing for an imminent ground attack. Each man was given a M-16, bandoliers of bullets, 3 hand grenades, and 3 flares. I was in my foxhole with some guy I had never seen before. Helicopters were flying everywhere and the tracer rounds looked solid red all night long. We never got attacked. As the sun came up, I looked over at the man that was with me and introduced myself as being from Augusta, Georgia. He replied, 'Chris Kune, Aiken, South Carolina.' We grew up 18 miles apart. Upon our return to Augusta, Chris, went to work for Delta Airlines as a ticket agent. I went to work traveling on an airplane every week for Johnson & Johnson. We have maintained our relationship for 48 years. He is a very dear friend.

"September 13,1969 was my last day in Vietnam and my birth-day. George and I got on the 'Big Bird' to head back to the world. They started calling a number of people off the plane to allow seating room for people going home on emergency leave. George and I made an agreement that if one of our names was called, that both of us would get the plane. Neither Grant or Hawes were called, so we were ready to go. You could not believe the appearance of some of the Marines that got on the plane. They looked like they had not had a bath in weeks and stank to high heavens. The first leg of our trip home was from Da Nang to Yokota AFB, Japan. As the plane was screaming down the runway, everybody was screaming their guts out. The stretch 8 was so full and loaded that it barely made it off the ground.

"Up, Up and away we go. Next stop Tokyo. I have not, to this day, witnessed the excitement and enthusiasm that was present on that plane. The American stewardesses were the most beautiful things I had ever seen. After 5 hours at Yokota, we finally were ready for the long leg to America. As we were taxing out to take off the pilot comes on and says, 'Gentlemen, we are now in a 30- minute hold, as a group of B-52's is coming in from a bombing mission from Vietnam.' The pilot had to cut off the engines and out went the air conditioning. Not a pleasant experience. Finally, after 45 minutes, the engines started up and we took off for the states. After we were airborne, the pilot again came on and said, 'Well Gentlemen, you might as well sit back and relax because it is a 13- hour flight to the mainland. If we run out of gas, we will have to stop at Travis AFB in San Francisco to refuel before continuing on to Norton AFB in San Bernardino. Guess what, we ran out of gas. They only let the emergency leave guys off. Finally, after 2 hours we took off. Just as the sun was coming up on September 13,1969, I remembered this was the only time I had two birthdays in the same year. One was in Da Nang 24 hours earlier, and now   because we had crossed the International Date Line.

"George and I were met at the base by one of his friends, who had come home earlier. We headed for Long Beach, California. I kept saying stupid stuff like look at the cars, look at that red light and finally look at that McDonalds. When we arrived at his friend's home, there was a flushing toilet, a shower and a television. Things we hadn't seen in 12 months. You don't know how much you appreciate something until you don't have it! His friend later took us to the Naval Station at Long Beach, where we would be released from active duty in 3 days.

"Remember what I said earlier; that not passing the OCS test would end up being the biggest blessing in the world for me. I only had to serve 15 months active duty, not the 4 years if I had become an officer. This allowed me to meet the most beautiful and wonderful love of my life, Victoria Burt, from Thomson, Georgia.

"We met on June 20, 1969 and were engaged 3 weeks later. I will never forget talking to her father to ask for his permission to marry Vicky. After about 3 hours, he finally asked me, 'Bobby, is there any special reason that you came to Thomson to see me?' "Yes sir, there is one question I have for you. Will you allow me to marry your daughter?" His answer was an immediate, "Yes" and "I'm going to bed!"

"Also, if uncle Broadus had lived, I never would have had the opportunity to meet Vickey. We have been married 46 years and raised two wonderful children. We are devoted members of First Baptist Church, Augusta, Georgia, and I thank God for allowing me to go through Vietnam without a scratch."

Hooyah!!!

Made in the USA
Columbia, SC
12 December 2017